Kings Town Publis

Snakes and Losers

by

Alfie Robins

Kings Town Publishing

British Library Cataloguing in Publication Data

A CIP catalogue record for this book is available from the British Library

ISBN: **978-0-9927594-1-4**

Cover photograph copyright of Tim Everett Photography, 2013.

Timeverettphotography.blogspot.com

Acknowledgements

Once again, special thanks to my family for their encouragement and support during the process of writing this book.

My daughters for keeping me pointed in the right direction, my son for cheering me up when the writing was tough and my wife for putting up with me constantly going on about characters and plots.

Also I would like to thank Barbara and Michael Morton for the help they gave in getting this book ready for publication.

For my daughters

With love

Snakes and Losers

Chapter 1

A crappy looking, dark blue and rust coloured Ford Transit van, the type with a sliding door on the passenger side, was parked up at the junction of Central Street and Cumberland Street. The fact that no overhead street lights were working was an advantage. The Council didn't bother repairing damaged street lights anymore; the "toms" just lobbed bricks at them as soon as they were fixed. What was the point of wasting tax-payers money? The dark night was perfect for what the three men in the van had in mind.

'Won't be long now,' Ian "Andy" Anderson said to his two mates, John "Finchy" Finch and Chas Logan. 'The club's empty. He usually comes out with one of the bouncers.'

Finchy was sweating. He was one of those people, who when you shook hands with them, you wanted to wipe your palm down your trousers. 'What if the bouncer decides to walk to the car with him?'

'Oh stop being such a tart,' Chas muttered as he leaned forward between the front seats from the back of the van, trying to see through the steaming up windscreen.

'He always follows the same routine. They come out of the club together, the fat bugger of a bouncer will carry on walking down Cumberland Street, while that dickhead Murphy will turn down Central and go right passed us to get his motor.' Anderson sighed, wishing he'd never brought the whinger along. 'Chas, how many times have we gone over it? It's a piece of piss, simples.'

'It's alright for you to say *no problem*, he doesn't know you. If he gets an eye full of my face I'm well and truly up shit creek.' Chas was starting to panic and sweat more than usual. He was as nervous as a vicar in a brothel.

'Well just make sure he *doesn't* bleedin' see you.' Anderson brought his hands up and covered his face in despair, muttering more obscenities into his palms. 'Ok, ok, one more effing time. He comes around the corner, they say good night and the bouncer carries on walking down Cumberland. That's when we put on the ski masks. Alright so far?' They nodded. 'Next, I've got my head down, right? As soon as he's alongside the van I jump out of the passenger side, grab him around the neck from behind, you two come out and give him a going over. I grab the brief case and away we go - a piece of piss.'

The tension was mounting. The smell of fear, stale sweat, burger wrappers and booze cloyed the air in the van. As Anderson predicted, they heard the bouncer shout good night and watched him head home. The two men went their separate ways, the bouncer walked straight ahead and Murphy turned left into Central Street.

'Get ready, put your masks on.' They did as they were told. When Anderson saw Murphy approaching the van he slid down in his seat out of sight.

Patrick Murphy, fifty eight year old owner of the *Snake Pit* Night Club had a BMI to die for – literally. He waddled his fat frame along the pavement, huffing and puffing, clutching his briefcase tight to his chest. The night's takings safely stashed inside. Anderson smiled. He was reckoning on lifting at least four thousand quid.

Murphy was 100 metres from the van heading their way. Anderson was impressed, the club owner was moving quite quickly for a fat bloke, 50 metres, things were looking good, 5 metres. The club owner hadn't seen Anderson tucked low down in the front seat of the Transit. Then the fat man was alongside. Anderson leapt of the van, grabbed Murphy from behind, kidney punched him and locked his forearm around the club owner's neck.

'What the feck...' Murphy grunted as an arm tightened around his windpipe cutting his voice to a croak. Finch and Logan bounded out through the van's sliding side door.

Whack! Logan swung the baseball bat into the club owner's fat gut. Murphy gave out an almighty gasping grunt. To say he was winded would be putting it mildly. He could taste the bile rising to his throat. Logan made a grab for the briefcase, Murphy wasn't having any of it and kept a tight hold, bringing it up and clasping it to his chest with both hands. Then the bones of Murphy's right hand gave an audible crack as the baseball bat found its target. The briefcase fell to the ground, along with his fat body. His face contorted in agony. Anderson loosened his grip around Murphy's neck, to save himself from being pulled over the top as the fat man toppled to his knees.

Finch was sweating like the proverbial pig inside his balaclava. Perspiration dripped down his face clouding his vision as it ran down into his eyes. He dropped to one knee and grabbed the briefcase. In a reflex action Murphy's good hand reached up for his attacker's face and a finger caught hold in the ski-mask eye hole. Finch flinched as he felt a fat porky finger stick in his eye. The mask pulled half away from his face. 'Ah, shit, shit, shit,' he shouted as he gave out another punch to the fat man's nose and yanked the mask back in place. Anderson grabbed the briefcase from Finch. For good measure he swung a well aimed boot at the side of Murphy's face making contact with the pudgy chin. Murphy lay quiet on the pavement.

Job done, unceremoniously the team bundled back into the van with Anderson at the wheel. He glanced in the rear view mirror at the bleeding lump of lard they'd left behind, Murphy's blood painted a dark liquid abstract picture on the pavement.

Anderson steered the van north up Cumberland Street, turned left at the junction of Fountain Road and headed for the safety of his own flat on Hull's Orchard Park Estate. An estate primarily comprising of social housing, it had been built to the north of the city in the 1960s, to house the many residents displaced by the west Hull slum clearance, in the once thriving fishing community of Hessle Road.

With one hand on the steering wheel, Anderson pulled off his mask and threw it into the foot-well. 'You pair of bleedin' morons, three against one, a useless fat bastard at that, and still you couldn't handle it.'

'Keep your knickers on, he never saw me,' Finch lied through his teeth. 'Got the money 'aven't we, stop the moaning.' Finch yelled back as he pulled off the ski-mask and wiped it over his sweating face.

'Will you two stop this crap 'til we get away from here?' Logan shouted, with his mask half way over his head. 'And for fucks sake watch the speed limit,' he added as he glanced at the speedometer.

***

'Well, are you going to open it or what?' The three desperados sat around the cluttered table in Anderson's dysfunctional kitchen.

'Just give us a minute, Chas, I want to savour the moment. It's not every day we get a payday like this.' He took a swig from his can of Fosters lager, burped loudly, put the can down on the Formica topped table and with the back of his hand he wiped the dribbling froth from his chin. His partners in crime waited with anticipation.

'Give us a can and stop fucking about.' Finch was fast losing patience. He reached across for a tinnie and pulled back the tab. 'Shit!' The beer spewed out over his hands. 'Come on, Andy. Get the fuck on with it.' They were desperate to see the contents of the case. They knew they were going to be in the money but not by how much.

Anderson stretched out his arms in front of him and flexed his fingers until the knuckles cracked. 'Hear that? It sounds like the bones in Murphy's hand as the bat hit it. Did you see his bleedin' face?' They all laughed. The tension was released.

'Ok here we go, ready for this?' Anderson was poised with his fingers on the latches. Click, another click and the lid sprang to attention. He stared at the contents, not looking up, not saying anything, he didn't smile he just stared into the briefcase.

'Oh for Christ's sake give us a look.' Finch couldn't stand the wait. He swung the case around, anxious to see the night's wages. 'Oh, shit.'

He pushed the case away as if he had burned his fingers on red hot coal.

Logan looked at their faces. He pulled the case towards himself, spun it around and looked inside. 'Oh shit,' he echoed. 'Now we're well and truly up shit creek.'

Amongst the bundles of used notes was an unexpected addition - a large package of Heroin. This was something the three amigos were not expecting, becoming the losers so soon.

Chapter 2

In the historic market town of Beverley some eight miles north of Hull, DCI Philip Marlowe stood on the towpath that runs beside the Beverley Beck, the mooring place of the *Daisy,* Marlowe's floating home. Marlowe looked at his watch. 'Oh no, not again,' he grumbled out loud, he was the only person on the tow path to hear his outburst. He was having a battle of wills and wit with his housemate, Archie a black and white dog of questionable parentage. Time was not on his side. 'Come on you little bugger I'll be late for work.' His patience was wearing thin. The mongrel took no notice and continued to scamper in the long grass along the river bank, in search of whatever he could find and doing what dogs do.

'About bloody time.' Archie bounded up, dragging what could only be described as half a tree between his teeth. Marlowe clipped the lead to the dog's collar and led him to his secure pen in the boatyard compound-come car park. 'See you tonight, pal,' he said as he locked him in. It wouldn't be long before Archie's mate, Harry, came to collect him.

DCI Marlowe once had a promising career in the East Yorkshire Police Force, unfortunately for Marlowe he'd crossed swords once too often with his superiors. Shipped out of Police Headquarters under a cloud, he was banished to the Gordon Street Police Station in the west of the city for a six month secondment. That was two years previous. Although no longer a favourite amongst the upper hierarchy, he didn't consider himself exiled to the wastelands in the least. The Gordon Street nick suited him down to the ground. He was pretty much his own boss and it meant he could run the CID department as it should be done, hands on with minimum interference from above. The station, built back in the Nineteenth Century, was a grey brick building with a grey slate roof and a working blue lamp above the door. Although the exterior of the Gordon Street nick was reminiscent of years gone by, inside, the station had been substantially refurbished and modernised to a high standard.

Marlowe drove his aging Ford Mondeo into the small nick car park. He was pleased to see no other vehicle in his allotted space. As he punched the security code into the back door of the station, he watched the arrival of his second in command, Detective Inspector Dave Gowan. The DI struggled to get his lanky frame out of his low sprung Audi. Marlowe smiled as Gowan tried to shake the creases from his already pre-wrinkled suit. He didn't stand much chance, it was well past its sell by date. But with a costly divorce looming, needs must, as they say.

'Morning, boss, how's it going?'

Marlowe stood by the station door holding it open. 'Good to see you back, Dave. How was the course?' he asked sarcastically, as he scratched at his head through his shorn grey hair.

'Now you are taking the piss,' Gowan replied, adding a 'sir' after a brief pause.

'Oh come on, Dave, you know you had it coming, there's nobody to blame but yourself.' DI Gowan was a good copper but had one major flaw, more often than not he would open his big gob before engaging his brain. Unfortunately for Gowan the last time it happened was one time too many, he had referred to an Iraqi gentleman who had been brought into custody as a "rag head". The trouble was the comment was said within earshot of Superintendent Bulmer. Bulmer, a stickler for rules and regulations had given Gowan the choice, an unfavourable comment on his record or a three day rehabilitation course, entitled, "Political Correctness in the Workplace". Gowan chose the latter.

'Come on, let's grab a coffee and you can tell me the latest developments in social whatsit.' Gowan shook his head as they walked towards the vending machine. Marlowe stopped, looked at Dave and then back to the machine, the DI took the hint and fished in his pocket for change.

Once Gowan had been relieved of all his loose change, they retreated into the DCI's glass cubicle of an office. The "gold fish" bowl had been built into a corner of the main squad room. To Marlowe's credit he had made it as comfortable as he could. Out of his own pocket he'd furnished the office with minor luxuries, a CD player, coffee table, small settee and a coffee machine with a mind of its own, hence the fact they were attempting to drink the diluted swill from the vending machine.

Marlowe pulled out his leather chair and sat behind his desk, switched on his computer and then leaned back with his arms clasped behind his head while the machine booted up. Dave Gowan dropped down onto the small sofa making the springs squeak, his long legs stretched out in front took up all the spare floor space. 'So, have you learned your lesson?'

'Oh yes,' replied Gowan, 'always check the Super's not around when you open your trap. Now if you're finished taking the piss, boss, I'll have a catch-up with Callum.'

'You'll have a job on, he's back north of the border in the land of the haggis.'

'How come, he hasn't been with us five minutes?' Callum McCraig had recently filled the vacant post of Detective Sergeant.

'Family crisis, the cat died or something.'

'That's great, so we're a man down again,' Gowan protested. The conversation continued with mainly small talk, Gowan moaning and groaning over the events of the previous three days. The arrival of Marlowe's long standing friend, Desk Sergeant Trevor Cleeves, put a stop to their banter.

'Magnum, you'll never guess who was...' Cleeves interrupted. Magnum, Colombo, Morse, P.I. or any other television police officer's name were all in Cleeves vocabulary, and always used in reference to the DCI. Often Marlowe cursed being named after Philip Marlowe, the fictional American private eye. The fact that Cleeves was one of Marlowe's oldest friends was the only reason he could get away with it. If anyone else tried, they did so at their own risk.

'Trevor.' Marlowe cut him off. 'Come in why don't you, just burst in without knocking like you usually do,' he said sarcastically. The comment went right over the thick skinned Sergeant's head.

'I did knock. As I was saying, you'll never guess who was done over last night.' Cleeves leaned against the door frame. Marlowe settled back in his chair, he knew from experience that the story was more than likely to be a long one.

'I haven't had chance to see the over-nighters yet, but I suppose you're going to tell us anyway.' Marlowe leaned forward with his elbows on the desk, waiting.

'Patrick Murphy, he got his head kicked in,' Cleeves said with a broad smile on his face.

'Yes! That is a result. Just what the Irish Bog Trotting Bast....' Gowan was interrupted as Marlowe tut, tutted and shook his head.

'Dave, think before opening your big gob, you've already been up to your neck in the mire.' Marlowe said referring to the event that had led to Gowan's so called *rehabilitation* course.

'Well let's be honest, boss, it couldn't have happened to a nicer feller. It's about time he was given a taste of his own medicine.'

Patrick Murphy was a big pain in the arse as far as the city's police force was concerned. Not only was he the owner of the drug dealers paradise called the *Snake Pit* night club, he was known to more than dabble in protection, prostitution and the importation and supply of Class "A" substances. All told he was a general racketeer of the old school. If you needed someone topped or knee-capped he was the man to sort it, for a price, there was always a price. Murphy did nothing for *gratis*.

'Did I disagree?' Marlowe replied and then turned to face Cleeves. 'Nothing that wasn't serious I hope?' He said with a broad smile on his face.

'Bad enough, it's going to put him the Infirmary for a couple of days. Broken hand, cracked ribs, oh yes and his gob's been temporarily wired shut, they reckon his face is as fat as a watermelon.'

'He is a fat sod anyway.' Gowan just couldn't hold it in.

The Sergeant chuckled to himself as he turned to leave. Then he just couldn't resist. 'That a new suit you've got on, Dave?' Cleeves made a hasty retreat laughing even harder.

'Piss off, *Sergeant*,' Gowan shouted as he self-consciously tried to smooth wrinkles out his trousers. They could hear Cleeves laughing his way along the corridor.

Marlowe once more assumed the position, lying back in his chair with his hands behind his head. 'Tell you what, Dave, I wouldn't like to be in the shoes of whoever did Murphy when his blokes get a hold of them.' He sat forward, picked up his coffee, sipped and spat it back into the cup. Rising he crossed to his coffee machine, turned it on and gave it a whack when the red light refused to turn green. 'Bloody useless thing.'

The DI untangled himself from the settee and stretched. 'If there's nothing pressing I'll go and have a word with the Irish gentleman concerned.'

'Just don't spend all day down there, take Jonno with you to get you up to speed on what's been going on.' Gowan raised an "as if" eyebrow and left.

As expected the usual suspects stood around the vending machine, the oldest and most experienced member of the squad, DC Johnny Johnson dropped a fifty pence into the slot as Gowan approached. 'Jonno, you busy?'

'Nothing that won't keep. Why?'

'Sort a pool car will you, we're going out. On second thoughts, I'll have one of those before we go.' He pointed towards Jonno's cup. Shaking his head Jonno slotted another fifty pence piece into the machine. 'You heard about Murphy?' Gowan asked as he waited for his drink.

'Oh yes, Cleevsey couldn't wait to fill me in with the details as soon as I walked in the station. There was a clang, hiss and spurting as the DI's plastic cup was filled.

Gowan picked it up, sniffed at coffee tainted with the aroma of oxtail soup and stood it on top of the machine. 'On second thoughts I won't bother. So, who do you reckon had the balls to do him over?'

'It has to be someone with cast iron underpants and balls of steel. Maybe Superman?' replied the DC. They both laughed knowing full well whoever had done the deed was either very brave or very stupid and definitely needed their head examined.

***

Jonno manoeuvred the Ford Focus pool car out of Gordon Street into the traffic. A left turn took them into the Boulevard heading for Hull Royal Infirmary on the Anlaby Road. They passed under the Anlaby Road flyover and the entrance to the KC Stadium, the joint home of Hull FC Rugby team and Hull City AFC.

'Good news about City,' Gowan said as they passed the stadium.

'Yeah, well let's hope they stay up longer than they did last time,' replied Jonno, referring to Hull City's recent promotion into the Premier League.

Five minutes later Jonno turned the car into the congested Infirmary car park, and parked up in the shadow of the towering 1960s structure. The scaffolding that had been erected from ground floor to roof, to hold the tiled facade in place for the past umpteen years. had finally been removed. At least now there was no fear of a facia tile dropping sixteen floors and decapitating some unsuspecting visitor. The interior of the HRI still had a long way to go as far as the refurbishment went, with tradesmen carrying out the renovations while the nursing staff did their best to do their duties.

'So, have you had much dealing with Murphy?' Gowan asked.

'Blood hell, Dave, I've known him since you were in short pants. I reckon I could write a book about the bloke. When he first came to Hull he had bugger all. He started out with a stall in Trinity market selling counterfeit jeans, knock-off gear and stuff like that. We never bothered so much about that back in those days, now look at the sod, God knows what he's into. On top of that we've now got that arse wipe of a nephew, Sean Keane taking a more up front role in the family business. We should have deported the pratt back to the Emerald Isle years ago.'

'Have we got an extradition treaty with Ireland?' Gowan jibed. Both men laughed openly and received a few strange looks.

'Any particular way you want to play this?' Jonno asked.

'No not really. Just want to see what state he's in, the fat twat won't tell us anything anyway.'

'You mean we've come all this way so that you can take the piss?'

'You know me Jonno,' said the DI, 'I care about all the citizens of this city.'

Gowan tried to keep a straight face but failed. 'Just like Batman.'

The two detectives showed their identification at the reception desk and were directed to the Orthopaedic ward on the seventh floor. At the nurse's station they again showed their identification. 'Are you sure this won't wait until tomorrow? Mr Murphy is still feeling a little poorly?' asked the nurse in charge, her eyes lingering a little too long on the DI.

Dave Gowan smoothed back his hair and flashed his best smile. 'It's vitally important we speak with Mr Murphy, we need to apprehend whoever carried out this vicious attack on him as soon as possible.' All the time he was speaking he stared into the nurse's eyes.

'Well, when you put it like that, I don't suppose a short chat will hurt.' Her cheeks flushed as she looked into Gowan's face.

'A chat, that's all we want.' He winked at Jonno.

'You smooth talking bugger,' Jonno whispered to the DI as they were shown to Murphy's room. Gowan tipped his colleague another wink.

'Still got it haven't I?'

Jonno just shook his head at the response of the younger man.

The club owner was in a private side-ward. Gowan opened the door without knocking. The room was classy, with quality furnishings and Monet prints on the wall. Had it not been for the medical equipment it could have been an expensive hotel suite.

'Better than some hotels I've stayed in,' Jonno said under his breath. Murphy obviously considered he was a cut-above the hoypoloy. The Irish gentleman wasn't the sort who would want to socialise with the common people on a communal ward.

The tub of lard was propped up with fluffy pillows, not the rubbery type found on the public wards, but the feather filled luxury type. His swollen face was definitely fatter than usual, his right arm was in a cast and supported across his chest in a sling. It was obvious he'd been dozing, by the way he jarred himself awake as Gowan and Jonno barged in, slamming the door behind them and making the glass rattle in the frame.

'Patrick, it's good to see you're looking so well,' Jonno said sarcastically as they stood facing the man in the bed. 'Do you know DI Gowan? Yes of course you do.' He dropped down onto the bedside chair. Reaching across he helped himself to a couple of the obligatory hospital grapes. 'Do all private patients get these?' Murphy gave him an icy glare.

'No, don't get up.' Gowan said as he motioned with his hand. He proceeded to sit down heavily on the edge of the bed, much to Murphy's annoyance.

The fat man in silk pyjamas looked as if he'd gone ten rounds with Joe Frazier. 'Ot da eck do u gont?' He mumbled through his swollen jaw.

'Sorry? Didn't catch that, you say something or do you have wind?'

The fat man on the bed looked furious. 'Piss off.'

'He said that clear enough,'

'I bet you he's been practising,' Jonno said to the DI in the one sided piss taking. 'Now, now, Mr Murphy, calm down. No need to be like that.'

'Patrick, have you any idea who attacked you? Is there anyone with a grievance against you apart from half the population of Hull?' Jonno reached across for more grapes and stuffed them in.

'Go to gell.' Murphy mumbled.

'Does that mean you don't know who we should send a "thank you" card to?

Murphy made a growling sound.

'I think he told us "to go to hell".'

Murphy glared, shaking his head.

'It's a bit like listening to a ventriloquist who's lost his dummy.'

'And a bad one at that.' They both laughed.

Gowan and Jonno carried on with their banter a little while longer before Jonno put on his caring face. 'Now let's be serious, Patrick, who should we thank for putting you in here?' They knew there was no point in being serious with Murphy. They wouldn't get anything out of him, even if he could speak properly.

'Eck off,' mumbled Murphy who sat fuming in his bed, gesturing with his good arm for them to leave.'

'Well if you're not *oing* to tell us anything we might as well *giss* off and leave *ou* to it.' The DI stood up rattling the bed as he did so. 'I won't shake hands; I expect you're using your good one for the piss bottle.' He grimaced and made a show of wiping his hands down the side of his trousers.

'Don't you forget, Patrick, if you need anything…don't call us.' Jonno added as he grabbed the bag of grapes and stuffed them in his pocket. The door slammed in the frame as they left.

'Gastards!' they heard Murphy try to shout through the closed door.

Contrary to what the detectives thought, Murphy did have a good idea who was responsible for his physical suffering and more to the point who had stolen his money and merchandise, at least one of them. Unable to speak with any clarity he picked up his Blackberry and sent an email.

Chapter 3

It was stifling hot. The window was as wide open as it would go. The girl, who sat at her desk staring at the computer monitor, was finding it hard to concentrate on her work. The sound of traffic along Hessle Road didn't bother her, but today there was an added accompaniment to the traffic and it was getting right up her nose. There was a constant bang, bang, bang and she didn't know how much longer she could put up with the racket. The pulse at the side of her head pounded and throbbed, it felt as if it was trying to beat its way out to freedom through the skin. Enough was enough; she pushed back her chair, stormed over to the open window and called out to the workmen operating the pneumatic drill in the street below.

'Oi, you two, how much longer have we got to put up with this bloody racket?' No one answered. So she yelled as loudly as she could. 'How much fucking long…' Then sudden silence as she was overcome with embarrassment. Everyone within earshot heard the expletive and looked up at the window.

'No need for that language, luv, we're knocking off for our break in a bit.'

'The sooner the bloody better,' she shouted back into the street.

'Snooty cow,' he called back knowing she couldn't hear him.

She sat down at her desk once more, head in hands trying to concentrate on the spreadsheet. Then finally peace and quiet, as the hammering subsided into silence. 'Thank you Lord, bloody thank you,' she proclaimed with relief to the empty room

'Wot ya doin down there?' Gary Mason shouted down the hole in the pavement. Mason and his mate Alan Clarke worked for the Small Works Division of Hull City Council. The hole they were excavating was once the entrance to a subterranean ladies toilet, at the corner of the Boulevard on Hessle Road. The public convenience had been closed and the entrance sealed some years ago.

'Won't be long mate,' Clarke called back to street level, 'just wanna ave a skeg at summat.'

'Hurry up, pal, I need a piss.' He could hear his oppo shifting lumps of concrete about.

'You still there, Gary?' Clarke called back up the hole.

''Course I am you silly sod, where else would I be?'

'Think you better come down and have a look at this.'

'I'm pissing meself here, can't it wait 'till later?' Mason yelled back down the hole.

'Just get your arse down here, NOW.'

'Alright, keep your bloody hair on, give us a minute.' Mason erected an extra couple of safety barriers around the area they were working; he didn't want a bollocking over some member of the public falling down the hole and breaking a leg. 'Ok, what am I looking at?' Mason asked looking over his shoulder as he descended the short ladder.

'Over there,' Clarke pointed.

'Can't see bugger all for dust, give us your torch.'

Mason took the offered high powered lamp and shone it in the direction of one of the boarded up toilet cubicles. The plywood board hung slackly on its screws, most likely loosened off with vibration of the drill. Peering through the dust, he kicked the debris out of the way and followed the beam of light.

'See it?' Clarke asked.

'Too bloody right I do,' he replied as he looked at a brown boot. 'Give us your phone.'

***

DCI Marlowe was up to his neck in paperwork when his phone rang. 'Marlowe,' he said into the receiver.

It was Sergeant Trevor Cleeves. 'I know it bloody is, I rang your number,' said Cleeves. The men had been friends since school days, hence the familiarity.

'No need to get clever, you old bugger,' Marlowe responded. 'What can I do for you?'

'Well, I've got a cracker for you.'

Marlowe could almost see the Sergeant smiling down the telephone. 'Come on Trev, don't pratt about, I'm overflowing with reports back here.'

'You remember when we were kids there was that underground ladies toilet at the top of Boulevard? You know, with them thick obscure glass bricks in the pavement?'

Marlowe smiled at the memory. 'We used to try and look though them.'

'Never could though could we. Anyway, the Council are pissed off with the traffic lights at the Boulevard and Hessle Road junction forever conking out, so they decided to see if they can get at the electric cables without having to dig the road up. They thought they'd try and do it from underground. So they've gone and opened up the toilets to try and reach the cables, and low and behold what should they find? I'll tell you what, shall I? A brown leather boot in one of the stalls. How about that then!'

'Ok, Tommy Cooper, what's so special about a boot?'

'There's a foot in it.' Cleeves chuckled down the telephone.

'Sent someone down there?'

'What down the hole?'

'Trev, I don't have the time...'

''Course I have,' the Sergeant snapped.

'Don't get stroppy, I'll sort it.' Marlowe hung up the receiver.

Marlowe sighed. He could feel his damp shirt stick to his back as he settled back in his leather chair. He eased forward again and pulled the damp material away from his body. The air-conditioning was on the blink and there was barely any draft from the open window. Marlowe took off his reading glasses, dropped them to the desk and massaged his throbbing temples; it wasn't as if they didn't have enough on and now this. He scooted the chair back and crossed to stand with his back to the open window cursing at the lack of a cooling breeze. He abandoned that idea with a mutter and peered through the glass petition into the squad room, it was like the *Marie Celeste*. There was only one officer at their desk, DC Tanya Etherington and she was under as much pressure as the rest of the team. Marlowe thought a trip out and some fresh air might recharge his batteries.

'Tanya.' She looked up to see Marlowe standing in his office doorway.

'What can I do for you, boss?'

'Fancy a ride out?'

Tanya knew, *no*, wasn't really an option. 'Be glad to get out of here for a bit.'

'Right, see you outside in five. We'll go in my car.'

He never said where they were going.

***

DC Tanya Etherington, had joined Marlowe's team a few months previously from the nearby market town of Driffield, she wanted to try her hand at big city crime and wasn't disappointed. No sooner had she joined the squad a major investigation was initiated and she'd soon proved her worth, quickly becoming a valued member of the CID Department at the Gordon Street Police Station.

'Mind if I open the window, boss?' Tanya asked, with her hand already on the button as Marlowe pulled the Mondeo out of the car park.

'Aye it is a bit warm in here,' he replied opening the driver's side window at the same time.

Marlowe turned the car out of Gordon Street into the Boulevard, three minutes later they were at the Junction with Hessle Road. 'Just out of curiosity, where are we going?' Tanya asked.

'We're here.'

Tanya gave Marlowe a funny look as he drove the Mondeo across the junction, signalled and pulled the vehicle onto the wide expanse of pavement next to a patrol car, adjacent to the council excavation works.

'It seems the council are carrying out some excavation work to do some maintenance of the traffic lights,' Marlowe said as they parked up, 'and some bugger has found a leather boot complete with a part of its former occupant.'

'You do mean a foot? Bloody hell.'

'Got it in one, let's go and have a look.' Marlowe took out his cigarettes. 'Don't mind do you?' he asked. He lit up without waiting for approval.

'Bloody coppers,' someone said as they passed. 'Typical, park anywhere they bloody want.' Tanya gave him the evil eye, and the passer-by continued to grumble as he went on his way.

A young uniformed officer stood almost to attention as they approached. 'Right son, what's your name?' Marlowe asked the constable guarding the hole in the pavement.

'Havers, sir.'

'First name?

'Kevin, sir,' came the nervous reply.

'Right then, Kevin, are they the blokes who found it?' He nodded towards the two council workers leaning against the side of their van, drinking take-away coffee from plastic cups.

'Yes, sir.'

'You been down the hole?'

'Yes sir, just to double check it wasn't a hoax or anything.'

'And?' asked the DCI.

'And yes, it's real alright. I tried to get those two to go back down with me but I couldn't budge them, they said, and I quote, "we're not going back down that hole 'til the bloody things gone."' Both Marlowe and Tanya smiled.

After a brief conversation with the "Likely Lads", Marlowe and Tanya turned their attention to the gaping hole in the pavement.

'If yer goin down there yer best put these on,' Mason shouted above the noise of the traffic and passed across a pair of bright yellow hard hats.

What a couple of clowns thought Tanya, as she descended into the hole, with the oversized hard-hat flopping down over her eyes. Thankfully the climb down the ladder was a short one. For once Tanya wished she'd worn trousers for work that day rather than a skirt, she hoped the boss wasn't looking up at her knickers. She reached the bottom of the short ladder without mishap and looked around. The room, if it could be called a room, looked to be about 5metres long and 4metres wide, the floor covered in rubble, bricks and concrete. The second rate portable lighting did nothing to lift the gloom. Four toilet cubicles with boarded up doorways still existed along one wall. On the opposite wall the basins had been removed long ago, leaving gaping holes in the wall were the copper plumbing pipes had once been. Marlowe shone a borrowed torch up to the glass block ceiling and smiled to himself at the memory, then shone the beam in the direction of the stall furthest away. The plywood hung loose, sticking out between the ply and the side panel was a brown leather boot.

Marlowe held the torch and aimed the beam into the cubicle. 'Stick your head in there and have a shuffty.' Tanya took off her hard hat and squeezed her head into the gap between the plywood panel and cubicle partition. 'There's a bit more than a boot in here, sir... like the rest of the body.'

'Oh, Jesus Christ, just what we need.' Marlowe went back to the base of the ladder and shouted. 'Kevin, get one of them blokes down here with a screw driver, then get on the radio to the nick, tell them I want the Crime Scene team down here, as soon as.'

'I'm not bloody goin' down there,' Mason said in response to the PC's request and passed across the portable battery powered screwdriver to his work mate, Alan Clarke.

'Cheers for that,' Clarke said sarcastically as he took the offered tool and reluctantly made his way down into the toilet.

'Ok, Mr Clarke, get this panel off.' Three minutes later the panel had been removed and propped against the far wall. In no time at all Clarke was back up on the pavement, rolling a cigarette.

'Reckon we'd best call the depot and let them know what's goin' on,' Mason said to his mate.

'Just a few more minutes, let's see what happens, you know they'll only give us another job to go too,' replied Clarke. They both lit a smoke and waited for the detectives to climb back into the light.

DCI Marlowe and DC Etherington once again surfaced into daylight to await the CSE team. Tanya was dispatched to find a couple of coffees while Marlowe pulled out his Benson & Hedges, and went to have a chin wag with the "Likely Lads".

***

A half a plastic cup of foul watery coffee and three cigarettes later the CSE team arrived.

'Morning, DCI Marlowe.' The Chief CSE Karina Taylor said as she approached.

'Now then, Karina, how's it going?'

'Not too bad, sir...careful with that equipment,' she yelled when some bugger dropped an aluminium instrument case to the floor. 'What have you got for us?' She asked as she watched her team with eagle eyes as they unloaded their equipment from the van. Marlowe gave the Chief CSE a run down on the events so far. Karina climbed into her protective forensic suit and over-shoes. She tucked her shoulder length blonde hair into the hood, put on her face mask, and with torch in hand she climbed down the hole.

Marlowe looked round at the surrounding buildings, the memories came flooding back. The area had hardly changed in the past fifty years. 'I was brought up around here, the next street in fact, Walcott Street.'

'So this is your old stamping ground, boss?'

'You could say that. Me and Sergeant Cleeves spent a lot of time watching the girls along here. Him, being a bit older than me, led me into all sorts of bother. I remember one time me and Cleevesy...on second thoughts, I'd better not tell you that one.'

Tanya now had a completely different picture forming in her mind of the boss and the overweight ageing desk Sergeant, an image of Beatle haircuts, bell bottom jeans and flowered shirts. She smiled to herself as they both crossed to the edge of the hole.

'How's it going down there?' Marlowe shouted down into the floodlit entrance.

'Why don't you get suited up and take a look?' Karina called back.

Once they had struggled into their protective forensic suits with the hoods drawn up, Marlowe and Tanya once again descended the ladder. There was hardly any room to manoeuvre, flood lights with wide spread tripod feet nearly took up all of the floor space. Marlowe stood in the middle of the debris and looked up, the obscure glass brick ceiling was still there, covered in multi-layers of tarmac. He couldn't help wonder to himself how on earth had he and Cleeves ever hoped to see inside.

'Karina, please tell me it was a natural death?' Marlowe mumbled through his protective mask, as he and Tanya looked over the CSE's shoulder into the cubicle. He knew it was a ridiculous notion. He'd been hoping it was some unfortunate dosser who'd passed away peacefully.

'Would be nice wouldn't it? But then again what would be the fun in that?' This was a good case by Karina's standard, no eyes to put her off, although she loved her job, her big phobia was looking closely into eyes, especially eyes of the dead.

Marlowe and Tanya watched as the CSE expertly worked the immediate scene. They could see that the brown booted foot had become separated from the rest of the leg. It looked like the tibia had come away from the ankle and a grimy bone was sticking out from what was left of a pair of denim jeans. The rest of the skeleton looked to be intact, or at least what was visible. From the waist up they couldn't be sure, the torso was covered in rubble,

Tanya leaned in closer. 'What do you think happened, I mean, you know with all that rubble on him?'

'Looks like a collapse of some kind.' The CSE leaned in for a closer look.

'Why on earth would a wall have collapsed on top of him? What was he doing down here in the first place?' Tanya asked.

'Digging a tunnel?' Karina said as she turned to face them.

'You are having a laugh surely?' Tanya said.

'Would I?'

Tanya knew full well she would, but not this time.

Marlowe scratched at his itchy stubbly hair, through the hood of his protective suit. He already had a good idea what might have happened. 'Tanya, go back up top, look around and come back down and tell me what you see.'

Even more puzzled now, she did as she was bid. At the top of the ladder, Tanya did a slow 180 degree scan of the area taking it all in, then the penny dropped. It didn't take long and she was back. 'Bloody hell, boss, there's what used to be a Midland Bank, not more than 6 metres away.

'Exactly. As Karina rightly surmised - digging a tunnel.'

Chapter 4

Sergeant Cleeves looked up from his paperwork as Marlowe and Tanya walked into the custody area. 'Bet that brought back some memories. You finally got to see inside the toilets.' Marlowe gave him the finger.

'Take a seat, Tanya.' Marlowe said as they entered his office. The DCI crossed to his coffee machine, gave it a thump and the machine gurgled. 'Works every time...nearly.' He poured two cups from the machine. 'Black, ok?' He passed one over without waiting for her reply.

This was a first for DC Etherington, coffee in the inner sanctum, she was well pleased. 'Do you really think this has something to do with a bungled bank job?'

'A tunnel, a bank a few metres away and a body, yes I do.' Marlowe picked up his mug and paused. He wanted to see Tanya's reaction and waited for her to take the initiative.

'I'll get in touch with council and see when the entrance was finally sealed, that should give us a starting point and the approximate time of death.'

Good girl, thought Marlowe. 'I know a fair few years have passed, but a lot of the businesses have been there a long time, start canvassing those in the immediate area you might dig something up, no pun intended.' Tanya had been with the team for around three months, she knew how Marlowe worked the squad, and was well pleased with what he said next. 'I'm going to let you run with this one, you ok with that?'

'No problem, boss.' Tanya was inwardly smiling and ready to burst with pride.

'DI Gowan is back from his course but if you need anything while he catches up there's DS Bright, and tell DC Kristianson he's working with you. Let's see if we can find out who the poor bugger is...was. I'll have a word with Sergeant Cleeves see if he can spare a couple of uniforms to help with the door to door.' Marlowe picked up a file; it was Tanya's cue to leave.

Tanya left Marlowe to his paperwork and went in search of DC Lee Kristianson, it was nearly lunch time and she had a pretty good idea where to find him. Kristianson had until two weeks before been the squads Trainee Detective. The young policeman had worked hard and on completing the statutory assessment period, along with passing the Detective's written examination, Kristianson had been awarded the full rank of Detective Constable. Tanya followed her nose which led her to the station canteen and, as she expected, to the young DC.

Although a vegetarian, Tanya still relished the smell of bacon sizzling away on the griddle. As hard as it was she fought temptation and settled for herbal tea and a buttered tea cake. 'I knew I'd find you filling your face,' she said as she sat down with her snack. 'How long have you been in here?'

'Ahh come on, Tanya, I've only just sat down,' he said lying through his teeth.

She grimaced at the stains on the table in front of her, taking a tissue from her shoulder bag she wiped the table top clean, once it was ketchup free Tanya sat forward in her chair resting on her elbows. 'You can be a right lazy sod at times. I bet you've been here filling your face since I went out with the boss.'

'You've been out with the, PI?' A term Lee used carefully, he had slipped up within hearing distance of the DCI and suffered Marlowe's wrath. 'A date? Kind of going out?'

'Grow up will you.' Tanya snapped. 'We've got a job on.'

'Not another missing dog. That's all I seem to get lately. That and old ladies who've lost their purses.' In a manner of speaking it was true, as the newest recruit he'd been getting the trivial cases.

'Not this time, a body's been found on Hessle Road.' Tanya sipped the herbal tea and watched Lee's face light up. It was a picture.

'A murder? The young DC asked enthusiastically.

'Suspicious to say the least.'

'A murder? and you're running it?'

She nodded proudly. 'And you're working with me, so let's finish our food and then you can get your arse into gear.'

'Yes, Ma'am,' he said, smartly throwing a mock salute.

***

The lack of circulating air in Marlowe's office was seriously affecting his concentration, the result of which left him with only one option, a smoke break in the fresh air. The station car-park at the rear of the station was a proper sun trap. Marlowe, top shirt button unfastened, tie loosened off and shirt sleeves rolled to the elbow stood enjoying the afternoon sun, chewing the fat with Sergeant Cleeves.

'Give us a light, Phil.'

Marlowe passed across his lighter.

'Cheers.' Cleeves lit up his rollie.

Marlowe was quiet, deep in thought. 'A bloody tunnel.'

'You what?' Cleeves said with blue smoke flowing from his nostrils.

'The skeleton, you know down in the ladies toilet. It looks like someone was attempting a bank job on the old Midland Bank, digging a tunnel.'

'Well I never, I thought it was just some tramp who'd popped his clogs...It's bloody warm out here.' He lay back against the wall with his face turned up to the sun.

'Mmm.' Marlowe took a drag of his B & H.

'Got to admit it, Phil, it takes some bloody nerve digging a tunnel right under everybody's noses.' He gave another pull on the roll up that was stuck to his bottom lip. 'Who've you put on it?'

'DC Etherington, Tanya, I told her you'd give her a couple of bods for door to door.'

'I'll sort it. Could just do with a lager, I'm right parched.'

'You and me both.' Marlowe stubbed out his cigarette in the sand bucket and left Cleeves with his face still turned up to the sun.

Back at his desk the paperwork seemed to be breeding of its own accord, *ok, so we're busy,* Marlowe thought and shrugged it off. It was nothing unusual to be snowed under, he had a good team who didn't knock on his door at every turn of events, they had proved themselves on more than one occasion, especially on their last case when one of their own went rogue.

***

Marlowe's drive home to Beverley was a long, hot one. As expected there was the usual slow crawl along the Hull to Beverley road. First he had to contend with the bus lane within the city limits. Then there was the mismatch of speed limits through the villages of Dunswell and Woodmansey, 30mph limit, into the 40mph and back into the 30mph, needless to say he was a little frustrated by the time he turned off the main road onto the tow-path for the last leg of his journey.

Home for Marlowe was a seventy feet long narrow boat named the *Daisy*, which was permanently moored alongside the Beverley Beck tow-path. Following his divorce the *Daisy* was all he could afford without tying himself down to a lifelong mortgage, something he didn't fancy at his time of life. After umpteen years of marriage his wife called it a day, no longer able to put up with the police lifestyle of late nights, the drinking and the fact that he was never at home. She'd told him "you love that bloody dog more than me." He never disputed the comment. Eventually push came to shove, and she'd run off with Shag Pile Charlie.

For Marlowe the boat was perfect, although only seven feet wide across the beam, the boat had every compact miniature built-in appliances he could want and was even connected up to all the on shore mains services. All in all the *Daisy* was easy to maintain and very economical for his needs.

Marlowe had adjusted well to being single again and was happy with his copper's lot. The one good thing to come out of the marriage was that he'd managed to be granted custody of Archie. Since moving into the narrow-boat Marlowe had become close friends with retired couple, Joyce and Harry who lived in the Old Lock Keeper's cottage. They had become Archie's unofficial adoptive carers. Rain or shine, all year round, Harry would collect Archie from the boat or his secure pen in the morning, take him for long walks along the tow-path and generally spoil him rotten.

Harry wouldn't admit it but he enjoyed the respite from domestic bliss with Joyce, and to some extent they had adopted Marlowe too. Harry, a retired sheet-metal worker was always eager to do the odd jobs around the boat that needed attention. And on more than one occasion Marlowe returned home to find a hot meal in the galley oven.

Marlowe turned the Mondeo onto the narrow tow-path, crunching gravel beneath the tyres. Archie had no problem recognising the distinctive sound of the car's rough engine as it pulled into the owner's compound. His four legged companion was eagerly waiting and wagging his tail when Marlowe opened the hatch. Archie danced around Marlowe's feet as soon as he stepped down into the small galley. He reached down and patted the dog, topped up his water dish and watched as Archie lapped the dish dry. Following another hot day in the office he felt the need to stretch his legs and reached for Archie's lead. 'Come on, pal, let's get some air,' the dog didn't need telling twice and hopped up the three steps to the aft deck. With the flexi-lead attached they set off for a wander down the tow-path.

The early evening was still warm with a gentle breeze coming off the beck, two hundred meters down the path near the lock gates, Marlowe perched himself on a mooring bollard and took out his cigarettes, while Archie stretched his lead to the maximum and did the sniffing and peeing thing in the long grass.

Back on board the *Daisy*, Archie was duly fed and watered. Checking the fridge was Marlowe's next priority. As usual there was next to bugger-all to entice his taste buds, apart from the half bottle of Australian Merlot left over from the previous evening. The copper's friend beckoned. Something from the freezer - along with the wine, of course.

***

The sun's rays penetrating through the overhead skylight woke Marlowe from his sleep long before the alarm was due to disturb him. It was 5am. His head throbbed from sleeping deeply. His back was stiff from sleeping on the dinette cushions, a habit he thought he'd got out of. He eased himself into the standing position and stretched until he felt and heard the vertebra in his back click into place. Once mobile enough, he let his pal out to do his business. Archie was always his first priority.

The kettle was duly filled and put on to boil while he headed for the built-in shower cubicle in the bedroom. After the hot water had done the trick of reviving his aching limbs, he forced himself to carry out a few more stretching exercises until he felt somewhere near human again. The early morning sun was streaming through the galley skylight, so with mug in hand and cigarettes in his pocket, he and Archie had breakfast on the aft deck. Marlowe sat in the sunshine and contemplated the day ahead while Archie wandered about the tow-path.

The one advantage to waking up early was that he would be in the office before the rest of his team. It didn't do them any harm to let them see he was on the ball. The DCI secured Archie in his pen to await collection by Harry. By 7.30am he walked into the station, he wanted to crack on with the neglected staff appraisals that should have been forwarded to Headquarters two days previous.

To the DCI's surprise, Detective Sergeant Jenny Bright had beaten him to it. 'Suppose I'd better get *you* a coffee, Jenny,' he said as he entered the squad room.

'Cheers, boss, never turn down a coffee.' Jenny had been staying with her sister and her husband for a couple of nights, to help out with the new baby. She'd been up since 4am due to baby duties, and by 7am work seemed the better option. She wasn't going to tell Marlowe the reason for her early start if it meant gaining a few extra brownie points.

'Anything in the overnight reports?' Marlowe asked as he passed across her drink.

'Haven't looked yet, boss. I'm just entering my notes from yesterday onto the system.'

'Bring your coffee and the overnighters through and we'll go through them.' Jenny nodded and followed him into his office. Marlowe saw another early bird entering the office, DC Etherington. 'And give Tanya a shout will you?'

The office door was open, all the same Tanya knocked on the glass panel. 'Morning, boss, sarge,' she said, smoothing back her hair as she walked in.

'Made any progress with skelly the toilet man?' Marlowe smiled. He thought it was funny even though his colleagues didn't crack their faces. 'Pull up a chair.' The DCI briefed Bright on the previous day's discovery in the ladies toilet and then handed over to Tanya.

'I checked with the Land Registry, the Midland Bank on the corner of the Boulevard closed its doors to business back in 1986, July 27th to be precise. The Council on the other hand closed the toilets in May prior to the banks closure. The entrance was permanently sealed about two months after the closure.'

Marlowe thought how the young DC was growing in confidence. 'I knew it was a long time ago, didn't realise how long. How was it sealed?'

Tanya glanced at her notes. 'Initially the door was just locked, a simple asp and staple job. Eventually a concrete slab was dropped over the stairs to seal the entrance.' She checked through her notes. 'That was on 13th August. A couple of months later the whole thing was covered over with tarmac.'

'That gives a window of just over two weeks,' Jenny chipped in.

Marlowe sat back in his chair, stretched his arms and folded them around the back of his head. 'Have you checked with Missing Persons?'

'I've left that with Lee to look into,' Tanya said as she stood up.

'Ok, chase him up when he gets in and keep us in the loop. Get us another coffee, Jenny, then we'll go through the over nighters.'

Tanya knew the routine and left them to it.

Chapter 5

'Are you are sure you want to discharge yourself, Mr Murphy?' The nurse in charge stood firm with her arms crossed in front of her.

The fat man attempted to pack his belongings into his overnight bag with one good arm. 'Look darlin', it's doing bugger all for me sat here in bed watching the friggin' telly when I've got businesses to run, is it now.' Murphy struggled with every word he spoke through his wired up broken jaw.

'Well, if you've made up your mind, you'll have to sign this self discharge form, but I strongly advise against it,' said the nurse forcefully.

'I'll sign any bleedin' thing you want, give it here.' Murphy scribbled his signature across the form. 'And why are you standing there like a flaming statue?' he said to one of the two henchmen who had come to collect him. 'Grab my bag and let's be off,' he growled in broken words. They got the message. With his jaw wired, his arm in a fibreglass cast secured across his chest and not forgetting the elastic bandages around his ribs, he still managed to walk two paces ahead of his employees as he left the hospital.

Twenty four hours after the attack Murphy was settled back in the comfort of his suburban home in the village of Ellerton, four miles west of the city. During his childhood, living in the slums of Belfast, Murphy swore one day he'd have a home to be proud of, and once he'd made his money he achieved his dream, a home in the country. A detached Victorian Villa standing in two acres of private land complete with stable block and paddock. Murphy lay back on the sofa, an Italian crystal cut tumbler, half-filled with ten year old Glenmorangie single malt whisky, in his hand. The first glass didn't do anything for him, but by the time he was halfway through the second glass, the pain began to lose its edge.

'Well, have you found the feckers who did me?' Murphy asked the young man who also sat nursing a tumbler of whisky. The club owner would have snarled had his face allowed him to do so. The pain may have been subdued by the pain killers and the whisky, but the temper was still as prevalent as ever. Sean Keane sat sprawled in the armchair facing his employer, Keane, six feet two inches tall and a snazzy dresser with it, not only worked for Murphy but was his own flesh and blood, his sister's son. Keane took a gulp of the whisky and smiled. 'From the smug look on your face I take it you have.'

'Sort of,' Keane replied edgily.

'Sort of, have you or haven't you?' Murphy was near the edge of his patience.

'Finch, the one you recognised, we've got him, Uncle Pat.'

'You've got him? Exactly where have you got him?' Murphy mumbled excitedly through his teeth.

'In the club cellar,' Keane answered proudly.

'My club cellar?' His face turned an angry shade of red.

'Who else's cellar?' Keane sat back and stretched his legs out.

'Have you lost your feckin marbles, what if any of the staff go in there to stock up?'

'Calm down, Uncle Pat, it's Tuesday, the clubs' not open 'til Thursday there's no staff on. The cleaners had been and gone before we got there. Murphy nodded his agreement, since he'd been worked over he'd lost all perspective on time.

'Well don't just sit there, help me get up, I want to see what the little shite has to say for himself.'

'He won't be saying much at the minute,' said Keane as he helped his uncle to his feet. 'That fat fucking moron of a bouncer of yours knocked his fucking teeth out.'

'Well he'd better be able to tell me where my fucking money and merchandise is or he'll be missing more than a few teeth.'

As far as night clubs go, the *Snake Pit* was no better or worse than other night clubs in the city. A popular night spot with the city's young, especially popular on "student" night when the price of the drinks came down and the optics were replaced with cheaper and often counterfeit brands. During the daylight hours the place was like Hull's many other clubs, depressing, the un-glitter-glitter ball and devoid of the fairy lights. With each step Murphy and his nephew took through the club their feet squelched in the beer sodden carpet. 'Do we have feckin cleaners or what?' Murphy challenged the younger man.

'Why, what are you on about?'

'Because they obviously aren't any feckin good at their job. Look at the state of the place, it's a shit house.' He pointed to debris scattered about the place, and the empty glasses still spread about the bar top and tables. 'Sack 'em all.'

'Bit drastic, Uncle Pat, I'll have a word with the supervisor.'

'Sack 'em, get a new team in, alright?' He didn't expect a reply and didn't get one.

Keane shrugged his shoulders. He knew better than to argue with the older man when he was in one of his moods. In pain from the broken ribs, Murphy winced as he pushed open the door leading to the cellar, which was not really a cellar but a storage room at the back of the building. The fat bouncer was sitting on a beer crate and stood up as they walked in. Finch on the other hand remained seated. This was due mainly to the carpet tape strapping him to an old wheeled typist's type chair. He didn't look in the best of health, dried blood congealed around his chin and neck. His right eye was swollen and partially closed. It was turning beautiful shades of blue and black.

Something crunched under Murphy's feet, he glanced down at the floor, bits of what used to be Finch's teeth caught his eye, he kicked them away and spun Finch around in his chair then walked away. Grabbing Finch by the hair Keane brought the spinning chair to a sudden stop. Finch gave a loud grunt at the pain. Keane wiped away the handful of loose hair across Finch's shirt. Murphy who been leaning on a stack of beer crates for support was breathing heavily. He slowly moved to stand in front of Finch, lifted the man's chin up and looked into his swelling face. 'Has he said anything?'

'Not yet, Mr Murphy, but he will, he's reckoning to be a bit of a hard man but we haven't really got going yet, have we, pal? Spinning the chair around once more, he took aim at the moving target and his fist once again connected with the side of Finch's head.

Finch sat dazed as more blood ran down the side of his face. Known as a hard-man, he was determined to live up to his reputation as long as he could. He was resolute he would not grass his mates up regardless of the consequences. He'd taken a kicking before, after all when you mixed with the sort of people he did, you came to expect it now and again, but he was determined to keep things together. The money would be worth it as long as he kept his cool. What was a couple of days in hospital compared to the pay day they'd had? He just had to keep thinking about what he was going to spend the money on. Murphy would not win this one. Then Finch remembered the drugs, this was *not* going to go away.

'Finchy, lad,' Murphy said in an almost jocular voice, 'ya didn't think I'd recognised you did ya? Bit of bad luck on your part you little shit. As soon as I pulled the mask away I knew it was you, you little bastard.' He laughed as he suddenly kicked the chair. It rocked to the point of almost tipping over. 'I don't suppose you know where my money is?' Finch sat stiff and wide eyed, he shook his head from side to side, the sweat on his forehead sprayed in all directions. 'Do I take that as a no? Don't suppose there's any point me asking about my drugs then?' Finch shook his head again. 'Well I'll give you one more chance, I'm only going to ask you once mind,' his voice changed, it became menacing, low and even. 'Who were the other two blokes? Think carefully before you answer. Two minutes and counting, Finchy lad.'

I can do this, thought Finch, keep my mouth shut, don't drop the lads in the shit and they'll get the message, a few cuts and bruises and out of here by midnight.

The overweight bouncer waddled across the room, held his arms straight out in front of him cracking the knuckles of his fingers for effect. He looked down and smiled at his victim. He could see the terror in Finch's face, as he placed one fat hand on the top of his victim's head, the other under the chin and gripped, in a practised vice like hold.

Finch tried to wriggle free but couldn't break the grip that tightened even more as he attempted to shake them off. Keane's face broke into a broad smile at the prospect of what was going to take place. He was an expert, after all his Uncle Patrick was a good teacher. He took off his jacket and carefully folded it and lay it across the beer crates, put his hand in the right-hand side trouser pocket and produced a Stanley knife. He pushed out the retractable razor-sharp blade and waved the chrome tool back and forth in front of Finch's face. His eyes opened even wider as Keane touched the point of the blade against Finch's cheek. 'BOO!' shouted Keane, Finch jumped in his seat. In a reflex action he pierced his own skin against the blade. Blood ran down his cheek.

Murphy smiled. He nodded to Keane. The fat bouncer still held Finch's head preventing any movement, Keane walked behind the man strapped to the chair. Finch struggled. His eyes flicked from left to right and back again trying to see what was going on.

It was Keane's turn to do the nodding. As the bouncer increased his grip around Finch's head, Keane grabbed Finch's left ear and pulled it outward from his head. Holding the Stanley knife in his right hand, and with almost surgical skill, he sliced down. Finch screamed a silent scream, with his jaws clamped shut he was unable to express the shock vocally and he bit into his tongue with what teeth he had left. Blood flowed from between his clamped lips and down the side of his face. 'Oh yes,' Keane shouted as he waved the dissected ear in front of Finch's eyes, then carefully placed the ear on the floor in front of Finch where he could see it.

The fat bouncer relaxed his grip. Finch gave out a screaming gasp of air. 'Logan and Anderson, they've got your money and the gear, all of it. Please no more.' Finch pleaded and sobbed like a child.

'Good man, a bit late like, my patience has run out and so has you're time. You shoulda listened when you had a chance, you fecked it, you could'a saved yourself some pain if you'd opened your gob when you had the opportunity.'

The hands clamped around his head once more. Another muted scream as the right ear was amputated. Blood ran freely down both sides of Finch's face and down over the bouncer's hands. Keane retrieved the ear from the floor and held them both like trophies in front of Finch's eyes. With a sly grin, he slipped the pair of them in the distraught man's shirt pocket. Keane made a show of cleaning the blade and wiping the bloodied instrument across the shirt of the amputee, before retracting the blade and returning it to his pocket. Finch sat stupefied, crying out loud and as shock turned to pain, the tears ran down his face and diluted the running blood.

Murphy kicked the chair, assigning the strapped in Finch to the filth of the floor. 'Get shut of him,' Murphy said. 'Then go find the other feckers.'

Chapter 6

Marlowe looked up from the seemingly never decreasing pile of reports, appraisals and flotsam of paperwork. 'Tanya, Lee,' he shouted as the two young detectives passed by his office window. Tanya gave the door a knock and walked in. 'Do the honours, Lee, black coffee for me and whatever you two are having.'

'Typical,' Lee muttered under his breath, as he fished about in his pocket for change for the vending machine.

Marlowe, although an "old school" copper, was not one for brow-beating or belittling the new younger breed of police officers. As long as they did their job to the best of their abilities, showed initiative and respected their peers, he in turn offered respect and encouragement. The DCI waived a hand gesturing it was ok for Tanya to sit down. She chose a hard back chair rather than the DCI's office sofa. While waiting for DC Kristianson to return Marlowe kept the conversation informal with small talk. This was something Tanya found difficult to comprehend, at her previous station in the market town of Driffield, her previous DCI never showed interest in his subordinates, you were only called into the inner sanctum for a bollocking, whether it was deserved or not.

'Cheers, Lee, I hope you got this from the canteen and not that manky machine down the corridor.' The young DC passed across his coffee sheepishly. 'Right then how are things going with our skelly?' They both gave him a quizzical look. 'The bloke in the toilet.'

Out to impress Tanya took the lead; she opened the A4 note book she liked to use for keeping more detailed account of events. 'His clothes are definitely circa 1970s, the type that might have been worn by skinheads, you know high lace up boots, jeans turned up, that sort of thing.'

'According to the anthropological pathology report, the body had been there a number of years, approximately forty or so in his opinion,' cut in Lee not wanting to be out done, 'as you suspected, boss,' he added hoping to score a few brownie points. Tanya gave her partner a filthy look.

The rivalry didn't go un-noticed by Marlowe.

'Got an ID yet?' asked the DCI.

'Working on it, the remains were in no state to be recognised and there wasn't any obvious identification on the body,' Tanya said, getting into her stride.

'What is interesting ...' Lee tried cutting in again.

Marlowe held up a hand to silence the young DC. 'Carry on Tanya.'

Before Tanya had a chance to elaborate there was a knock at the door. Karina the chief CSE put her head around the corner of the door. 'Is it alright to come in?' Marlowe waved her across to a vacant chair.

'What can we do for you?' Marlowe asked as he settled back in his chair.'

'It's about the body in the toilet.'

'What about it?' He leaned forward on his elbows.

'It looks to me as if the cave-in was staged.'

***

During the few good summer weeks of the year, the car park of the Gordon Street nick came into its own as a sunbathing area. The temperature was well into the twenties. Sergeant Cleeves was already in the designated smoking area, sucking on a thin roll up when Marlowe decided to take a break. Marlowe slackened off his tie and unfastened the top button of his shirt. 'Bloody warm out here, Trev,' he said as he took out his own cigarettes.

'Too nice to be at work,' Cleeves replied laying back against the brick wall, turning his face up to the sun. 'Dave got over his course yet?'

'You know Dave, won't be long before he opens his big trap again and upsets somebody.' Marlowe took out a Bensons and Hedges and lit up.

'Give us that,' he passed over his lighter, 'I feel like sodding off home.'

'You having problems?'

'Na, just busy that's all,' Cleeves said slacking off his uniform jacket around his paunch.

'So what's new, it's the nature of the job.'

'Luggless Douglas, was brought into the infirmary.'

'Who the hell is Luggless Douglas?'

Immediately Cleeves brightened up and laughed like his usual self. 'Sorry, couldn't resist. I had two lads down at the infirmary, they'd gone to interview some old lass who'd been mugged in the city centre. Anyway a nurse collared them, they'd just had a bloke stumble in with his ears cut off, they were stuffed in his shirt pocket.

'Trev, don't you ever give up with the piss taking?

'No, for real this time...'

'Oh, for pity's sake, Trev, get on with it, who was it?' Marlowe was quickly losing patience.

'Finch, John Finch. He was the bloke with his ears in his pocket. It's a good job there's a fair bit of cloud today.'

'And why's that?' Marlowe asked.

'He wouldn't be able to keep his sunglasses on.' Cleeves almost pissed himself with laughing at his own joke. It took Marlowe all his time not to smile.

'You know what, Trev? I reckon you should suggest to Headquarters that they set up a nick inside the Hull Royal.'

'You know what, Phil, that might not be a bad idea at that.'

'What did Finch have to say for himself?' Marlowe asked.

'Not a lot, by the time the lads went to see him he was drugged up to the eye balls with pain killers and the like.'

'Talking about hospital visits, Dave Gowan and Jonno paid Murphy a visit the other day, didn't get anything out of him though. I think they only went to take the piss.'

'Discharged himself didn't he?' Cleeves took out his tobacco tin and rolled himself anther skinny cigarette, then passed the tin to Marlowe who shook his head in disgust, soggy roll ups didn't do much for him.

'So I heard. Let's hope his recovery is a long and painful one, keep him out of our sights for a while.'

Marlowe finished his smoke and reluctantly went back inside, leaving the Sergeant concentrating on blowing blue smoke rings into the air. Something unusual did seem to be happening, first someone brave enough to assault Murphy and then another poor bugger has his ears chopped off. *Now that is something Murphy would do*, thought Marlowe. On his computer he accessed John Finch's file. John Albert Finch, aka "Finchy", GBH, house breaking, possession with intent to supply, the list went on, he was well known to police across the city. His last incarceration at Her Majesty's invitation had been three months in Wakefield nick for receiving stolen goods, but there wasn't anything recent. Marlowe pondered for a moment or two, wondering who the poor sod had pissed off to warrant having his bloody ears cut off, could it have something to do with Murphy? There was no evidence to point that way, it was just a feeling he had.

***

'Hear about that little shit Finchy having his ears cut off?' Gowan asked Marlowe as he walked into the squad room.

'Trev was just telling me. Ouch.'

'It fair makes you wince...ugh, I don't know what he'll do when he comes out of hospital and it's a sunny day.'

'Don't waste your breath, Dave, I heard it all ready.' Gowan laughed alone. 'I know Finch hasn't officially reported it, that was down to the hospital," continued Marlowe "but have a sniff around and see if you can find out what he's been getting up to.'

'Jonno.' DC Russ Johnson looked up from his desk. 'You're with me again, another visit to the hospital.'

'Not again, what is it this time?'

'John Finch, some bugger has done some surgery on him, cut his bloody ears off.'

'Pardon? Jonno said, smirking.

'Somebody has... ha, ha, not funny.'

***

'Tanya, home time,' Marlowe said as he came out of his office, 'it's well past knocking off time, get yourself down the pub with the others.'

'I just need to finish this off, boss, save time in the morning,' she replied looking up from her computer screen.

'You do know there's no overtime don't you?'

'Yes, its fine, I won't be long.' The pub was the last place she wanted to be after a long day.

'In that case I bid you good night.'

'Night, boss,' she said, again tapping away at the computer keyboard. Ten minutes later, she sat back in her chair feeling pleased with the day's achievement, turned off the computer and headed for the door. Tanya had just about reached her car when her mobile sang at her, reluctantly she took it from her bag. The display read "Lee calling" *What now?* she thought. 'Lee, what do you want?'

'Tan, you coming for a drink?' She could just make him out above the din in the background.

'Lee...I can't hear you, too much noise.' All she could hear was shouting and music in the background.

'Listen I'm in the *George,* the Karaoke is starting in half an hour and the DI's put his name down, you coming?'

'Not tonight...you'd all be pissed by the time I got there anyway.'

'Aw, c'mon, Tan, it's heaving in here already, it'll be a good night.' He sounded over-excited.

'Lee, I've been up since six this morning, and I'm definitely not interested in listening to DI Dave Gowan doing his crap impression of a crap pub singer.' She couldn't make out the reply above the noise and hung up. Dave Gowan thought he was Hull's answer to Roy Orbison, Tanya remembered the last time the DI did his karaoke stint and she wasn't impressed. She was convinced that if the locals hadn't known he was a copper, he would have been arrested for noise pollution.

DC Etherington, had until recently been living at her parent's home in the market town of Driffield, some 22 miles away, until the excitement of the big city prompted her to apply for a transfer. With the daily travel from Driffield combined with the unsociable hours she was working of late, taking a rented flat seemed to be the logical thing to do. Tanya's one bed-roomed flat was on the third floor of a pleasant pre-war three story town house in the Avenue's area of Hull, with a good view of Pearson Park.

She pulled her Vauxhall Corsa into the kerb edge, locked the car and went into the house. Picking up her mail from the table in the communal hall, she trudged up the stairs to the third floor, unlocked her flat and went in. She hung up her jacket, kicked off her shoes and went through to the kitchen, and as the saying goes *the kitchen was bare*. Looking inside the refrigerator didn't help. A half bottle of white wine and a sad looking piece of cheese with green stuff growing on it stared back, as if it dared her to eat it. Tanya sighed, grabbed the wine bottle and slammed the fridge door shut. She turned and took three steps across her small kitchen and studied the local takeaway's menu pinned to the cork notice board. Decision made, she took out her mobile. 'Vegetarian fried rice and a couple of onion bhajis, please,' she said into her mobile, 'thanks, yes that's the address.'

Before her takeaway arrived, Tanya managed a quick soak in the bath to wash away the day. Feeling a damn sight fresher, wrapped in her towelling bath robe and with her takeaway on a lap-tray, she sat in front of the television watching yet another reality show. Meal finished and the wine bottle empty she sat looking around the flat. She had been living there three months and had yet to make her mark on the place. She took some colour charts off the unit and contemplated making a start on the re-decoration at the weekend if work allowed, but the thought didn't last very long, her bed beckoned. Like the new girl in school she felt she needed to impress the DCI and an early night was called for.

Chapter 7

'Chas, I'm in the *Vic*, get your arse down here double quick,' Anderson said into his mobile and hung up. The *Victoria* was, to put it bluntly, a dump of the first order. With a deco that had hardly changed since the 1970s. The surviving maroon flock velvet wallpaper was peeling at the edges, the paintwork yellowed and stained with nicotine, and the threadbare carpets hadn't been shampooed since they had been fitted. In short, the Victoria was a shit hole and a favourite haunt of small time villains, winos, dead beats and life's losers.

Ian "Andy" Anderson had already downed three pints before he made the call, still his nerves kept him wanting more. 'Billy, gimme a large whisky. ' He offered no please or thank you when the drink was put on the bar in front of him, just stood staring at the glass, then picked it up, downed it in one and slammed the empty glass back on the bar when Chas Logan arrived.

'Now then, what's all the panic about?' He nodded to Billy, who automatically pulled him a pint of lager and another whisky for Anderson.

'Have you heard about Finchy?' He picked up the whisky and sipped, this time he grimaced at the taste of the cheap liquor.

'No, not seen him since the other night, why?' Logan picked up the pint.

'I think we've been rumbled, grab that table,' Anderson nodded towards a beer puddled table near the door to the gents.

'Some bastard has put him in hospital,' he said in a low voice as he leaned across the table.

'Serious?' Logan asked. Worried now, he picked up the glass and took a deep swallow.

'Serious…he's only gone and got his fucking ears cut off!' His voice waivered.

'Jesus…Murphy?' Logan picked up his pint and finished it, before calling across to Billy to fetch more drinks.

'You are serious? Who the fucking else would it be? Do you know any other nutter who'd do owt like that?

'But fucking hell why his fucking ears?'

'Fucked if I know.' Anderson shook his head in disbelief. Inside he was shaking.

'We'll be alright, Finchy's sound as a pound, he knows how to keep his gob shut.'

'I hope you're right, I'm a bit attached to my ears!' Both men laughed nervously trying to release the tension of the conversation. Anderson shouted for Billy to hurry up and bring their drinks over.

'This time next week, Murphy will have forgotten all about it.'

'You reckon?'

'Course he will, we'll be fine I'm telling you.' Logan didn't really believe his own words.

'Yeah, well and what are we going to do about the drugs? I don't know anybody who'd buy that amount of stuff.'

'What do you reckon to this, we post it back to him anonymously like, it might stop him coming looking for us.'

'Fat fucking chance of that, you know what that animal is like, he'll want his pound of flesh or whatever.'

'Yeah, or ears.' They laughed again trying to make light of the matter. Inside, they both knew it was only a matter of time before Murphy's nephew came calling.

'Just keep it hidden away, I'll ask around.' Anderson knew that would be a waste of time, they didn't know anybody in the big league who would take it off their hands.

Anderson sat pondering for a minute or two. 'You know what I reckon?'

'What?'

'We sit here and get pissed.' More nervous laughter.

Chapter 8

The aroma of fried sausages and bacon greeted DI Dave Gowan as he walked into the first floor canteen at the Gordon Street nick. DS Jenny Bright sat with a bowl of muesli in front of her, nursing a mug of station coffee pondering on what the day would bring.

Gowan really fancied a greasy breakfast but thought better of it, there was no time. He grabbed himself a coffee from the counter and wandered across to where Jenny sat. 'What are you on with?' he asked interrupting her thoughts.

'I *was* enjoying my breakfast,' she lied, the cereal was bland and the coffee stewed. 'You must have had a good night judging from the look of you.' His creased suit looked more creased than ever.

'Just a night out in the *George* with the lads, it was a good do, you should have come.' Gowan fished about in his jacket pocket and brought out a blister pack of pain killers, he popped two paracetamol tablets into his hand and swallowed them back with his coffee. 'Tell you what, that young Lee is a good laugh when he's had a drink, he even had a go on the karaoke.'

'All the same…on a school night, I'd have thought you'd know better, you look like crap and smell like a brewery.' Gowan just shrugged his shoulders.

'Anyway, as I asked before what are you on with?' Gowan was still catching up on events while he'd been on his course.

'Not a lot, two break-ins, one with assault, a spate of organised shoplifting along Hessle Road, stolen credit cards, oh and keeping an eye on Tanya and Lee.'

'Not too busy then,' Gowan said as he smiled, 'I'm after a favour.'

'I might have known, and what is this favour, inspector?' Jenny asked sarcastically.

'Don't worry, it shouldn't take up too much time, I want you to have a look and see if you can find any link between Patrick Murphy and John Finch.'

'The bloke who had his ears cut off?' She was interested, no matter how busy she was.

'That's the one, it's nothing concrete just a feeling that it could have something to do with the working over on Murphy.'

'I'll do my best to fit it into my busy schedule, I'll get uniform to check into my some of my ongoing; they must have someone they need to keep occupied.'

'Cheers, Jenny, you're a star.'

'I know, but you can keep up the grovelling as long as you like. You will pay for this you know that don't you?'

'Yeah, probably twice over,' said Gowan.

'Anyway, how did the course go?' she asked smiling.

'Oh go on you take the piss as well, everyone else who dared has done.'

'As Del Boy would say, "He who dares wins". She smiled, turned and walked away.

**

Not one to waste any time, Murphy had Keane follow up on the information they had gleaned from Finch, not that Finch had had much say in the matter. It didn't take Murphy's nephew very long to find Chas Logan. He was a creature of habit, by eleven o'clock he would be in the betting shop, then into the *Victoria* for a pie and a pint.

Logan had already paid his daily visit to the betting shop, putting a fiver each way on some cert that was bound to come in unplaced. Standing at the far end of the bar, laughing with his mates and flashing the cash like he'd won the lottery, he reached for his pint amongst the bar full of dirty plates and cutlery waiting to be taken through to the kitchen.

Sean Keane quietly entered the pub by the back door leading from the car park. Un-noticed by Logan, or anyone else for that matter, he stood inconspicuously at the opposite end of the dog-leg bar and ordered a bottle of lager. From his vantage point he watched and waited. He wasn't in a hurry. Logan, completely unaware of the fact he was being watched laughed and joked with his cronies. After half an hour or so, Logan's hangers-on barring one, drifted away when they realised he wasn't going to stand them drinks for the duration of the afternoon.

Keane decided it was time and made his move. By now Logan was three parts pissed, but not so drunk he couldn't see Keane approaching. 'Oh shit,' Logan muttered under his breath. He could feel a nervous heat rising through his body up to his neck, *so much for it blowing over.*

'What's up with you, you look like you've seen a friggin ghost?' Logan's drinking buddy piped up.

'See that bloke coming across? I owe him some serious money,' Logan, lied full on.

'Don't worry mate, I'll sort him for you,' said the drinking buddy. *If only it was that easy*, thought Logan.

Keane approached, his eyes showing no emotion, he smiled through his thin lips. 'I'll have another bottle of lager, please luv,' he said to the bleach bottle blonde, middle-aged, overweight barmaid. 'Chas, how are things going?'

Logan didn't know how to respond. He didn't know if it was merely a coincidence that Murphy's nephew happened to call in the *Victoria* for a pint. Subconsciously Logan didn't think so. He reckoned he'd soon find out.

Keane watched the barmaid bend over the drinks cooler, her leggings riding down to reveal rolls of fat above her fat arse. 'Thanks luv,' he said when she put the bottle down in front of him. He paid for his lager, put the bottle to his lips and sipped before wiping his mouth with back of his hand. 'You hear me, Chas? I said how are things going?' Logan looked down at his feet and kept silent. He hoped the floor would open up and swallow him down into hell.

'Look 'ere mate,' said Logan's drinking buddy as he stepped around Chas and placed himself between the two men. 'He aint got any money, ok, comprehend, so why don't you just finish your bottle and fuck off out of it back where you came from?'

Oh shit, shit, shit. Logan was not far off from peeing in his pants, he looked straight ahead, watching in the mirrored wall behind the bar, he couldn't miss the twitch in the corner of Keane's eye, thing were going to kick off, he was sure of it.

'And who the fuck are you?' Keane demanded to know.

'I'm his fucking mate that's *who* I am, ok.' With bravado he stood his ground and placed his hands palm down firmly on the bar, defiantly.

Keane picked his lager and took a deep swallow, licked the froth from his lips and carefully placed the bottle down on the bar. He turned slightly to one side. With his right hand he picked up a dirty fork from a plate waiting to be taken to the kitchen and without further ado he raised his arm in the air and down again. The drinking buddy gave out an almighty scream as he looked down to see the fork sticking out of the back of his left hand. 'What ...what ... the ... fuck ... you do that for?' He asked in gasping breaths.

'Because what I'm here for's got fuck all to do with you, got it? Now you and your cutlery can FUCK OFF!' The man's face was a deathly shade of grey as he looked back and forth between Logan and Keane, the blood seeped out beneath the palm of his hand, he couldn't move it, the force had been such, that the prongs of the fork had pinned him to the bar top. 'I do mean now,' Keane calmly whispered into his ear

'B... but ...I ... can't move it!' he groaned almost sobbing. All the while Logan stood watching and waiting.

Keane picked up his bottle and swigged, holding the bottle by the neck he smashed it down on the edge of the bar, he held the sheared off glass neck against the man's face. 'Not my problem, Pal, right now I'm going for a piss and if you're still here by the time I come back ... know what I mean.' He pushed the glass gently into the man's neck; just enough to draw a slow trickle of blood. 'And you,' he said turning to Logan, 'don't you fucking dare go anywhere, hear me?' Logan was resigned, he wasn't going anywhere.

Keane took out his mobile as he walked to the gents, pressed the speed dial and spoke. 'It's me ... yeah I found him ... be with you shortly.' He hung up, had a piss, washed his hands and went back through to the bar. Logan was still there, dropping beer mats into the pool of blood on the bar.

'Come on loser, there's someone who wants to see you.' Keane reached out non-too gently, grabbed him by the arm and led him to the car. The fat bouncer sat in the driving seat. Through the open window he smiled, just like a Bond villain.

The journey from the *Victoria* to the nightclub took all of fifteen minutes, but for Logan sat in the rear seat of the car it seemed to last an eternity, or he wished it would. During the journey all he could think about was his ears and how he wanted to keep them. By the time the car came to a halt in the *Snake Pit* car park, Logan was really struggling to control his bowels, his stomach heaved, he was afraid one wrong move and he'd shit himself. The fat bouncer helped Logan out of the car by grabbing his collar at the scruff of his neck and almost frog-marched him into the club through the reinforced steel door. That's when Logan's bowels finally gave out. 'Oh, for fucks sake, you dirty bastard, and we haven't even started yet,' said Keane as he pushed Logan inside.

'Chas, please come in. Why didn't you show our guest to the toilet?' Murphy asked his nephew sarcastically through his broken jaw. Logan was wild eyed; his legs froze as he was ushered into the club storeroom piled high with crates of beer and boxes of crisps.

'Sit your shitty arse down there.' There was only one seat, the same typist chair that Finch had occupied. Keane put his hands on Logan's shoulders and physically pushed him down

'Won't keep you too long, just got a couple of questions for you.' Murphy wrinkled his nose at the stench emitting from Logan.

'But first,' he looked towards the fat bouncer who immediately punched Logan square on the nose, the cartilage cracked and the blood erupted as the skin split wide open, he fell to the floor in a heap. 'That, my friend, was in repayment for the injuries you and your cronies inflicted on me.'

Keane and the bouncer grabbed an arm each, hoisted Logan to his feet and then unceremoniously dropped him onto the chair. 'Don't fucking think about farting, never mind moving,' the fat bouncer said. He bent over and picked up a roll of carpet tape off the floor and started to bind their guest firmly in situ.

'Now to business,' said Murphy, 'where's my feckin property?'

Logan sat stiff backed, the tape securing him to the swivel chair held him tight, he couldn't budge an inch. When he did try to speak, it just came out as an incoherent garble through the thickening liquid escaping from his mouth and what used to be his nose. Murphy knew that Logan wasn't bright enough to be the brains of the outfit; he just wanted confirmation that Ian Anderson was the keeper of his money and goods.

Keane spun the chair around and around, Logan felt sick, it was like having a bad experience on the walzers at the annual Hull Fair. The bouncer stuck out his foot and brought the chair to an abrupt stop, Keane caught the chair before it had a chance to tip over.

Logan tried to move his head forward and failed. His stomach retched and he vomited not only over his own feet but also Keane's shiny shoes. 'You filthy bastard,' he muttered and gave Logan another thump on the side of the face. 'Have you seen your mate, Finchy lately?' There was no response from the man in the chair. His head still felt as if it were spinning, he couldn't speak even if he'd wanted to. 'No? Probably not, if you had you'd have known we've already had a little chat with your mate. They tell me he's a little hard of hearing at the moment.' Logan's eyes darted about the room crazily.

Murphy steadily walked closer towards the chair and nudged Keane aside with his shoulder, with legs splayed and his good hand in his pocket he stood directly in front of Logan. 'Now, are you going to be a good lad and come clean? Clean did I say? You've just shit your pants.' Everyone but Logan laughed. He was frantic. His eyes darted from Murphy to Keane and back again. He was terrified, he knew what Murphy was capable of, and he knew if it wasn't for Murphy's predicament, the club owner would be dealing out the punishment himself. The blood and snot continued to run down his face, as he splurted out to them what they wanted to hear. As they say he "sang like the proverbial canary".

Grassing up a mate was not a facet Murphy approved of. 'Mr Logan, thank you for being so forthcoming with the information, you snivelling, whining little twat, you should learn how to keep your mouth shut. Grassing up a mate like that, tut, tut. Well you *will not* be grassing up anybody else in the near future.'

Wild eyed, Logan thrashed about on the rickety typist chair, it rocked from side to side on its wheels but there was no escape, the tape held him firm. Not that there was anywhere to run. From the corner of his vision he saw Keane approaching, he was holding something in his hands. Logan tried to turn his head but the fat bouncer reached out with both hands and held his head firmly. He could feel his groin becoming warm and wet as the piss ran down his legs. 'Again,' said Keane as he looked down and saw the pool forming on the floor. 'You are such a dirty bastard.' Logan continued throwing himself about in his chair trying to make things difficult, he didn't know what punishment Keane had in mind for him but he wasn't going to make it easy for him.

Murphy, resting his aching body against a pile of beer crates stood watching the proceedings, he was fast losing patience, he wanted it over and done with, so he could get back home to the pain killers and whisky. 'For fecks sake, stop feckin about and batter him over the head or sommat and let's get on with it.' The bouncer didn't need telling twice, from the nearest crate he picked up a bottle of lager in his right hand, swung his arm in a wide ark and with much more force than was needed, the bottle smashed against bone, right behind Logan's ear. The blood gushed from the wound.

'I said feckin batter, not kill him you feckin idiot!' Murphy yelled.

The fat bouncer leaned close to Logan. 'He's still breathing. Look you can see his chest is going up and down.'

'Head wounds always look worse than they are,' Keane said with no compassion.

'Head wound! Head wound my feckin arse, that feckin idiot's caved the feckin thing in. Just get on with it.' Murphy reached into his jacket pocket, took out a miniature cigar and lit up. The small room filled with a hazy blue smoke that curled below the storerooms low ceiling.

For once luck was on the side of Logan, he passed out before his punishment had begun, and he stayed that way. It wasn't until he woke up in the Hull Royal Infirmary twenty four hours later when the feeling in his mouth came back, that he was then fully aware of what his punishment had been. His tongue was missing, along with half of his teeth. A nurse had found the lump of mangled flesh in his trouser pocket, there had been no chance of trying to reattach it.

Chapter 9

'The sun is shining, the birds are coughing and another little turd is taken off the streets,' Sergeant Cleeves said out loud as he walked across the station car park to where DCI Marlowe was having a quiet fag. 'Well Magnum, the day has started on an uplifting note.' Marlowe smiled, he knew a story was about to follow.

'Morning, Trev,' Marlowe said shrouded in a cloud of tobacco smoke. 'What are you so cheerful about?'

'Chas Logan, remember him?' The DCI nodded. 'Well he's been given bed and breakfast at the Hull Royal for a few days, not that he'll be wanting the breakfast or any other meals for that matter.'

'What on earth are you on about?'

'Logan, he met with a little bit of misfortune yesterday afternoon.'

'He's a mate of John Finch isn't he?' Marlowe recalled.

'The very same,' Cleeves took out his tobacco tin and skinned up a thin rollie. 'Anyway it seems he was dumped outside the Infirmary late yesterday afternoon and tried to crawl his way into A & E like a slug.' Marlowe was patient, as he watched Cleeves stick the roll-up to his lip and light up. As he knew Cleeves' stories did tend to run on at times, against his better judgement he lit a fresh Benson & Hedges from the stub he'd been smoking. 'It appears somebody just about caved his head in and … go on have a guess.'

'Stop pissing about Trev.' The Sergeant was a bit of a drama queen. Marlowe waited for the punch line.

'They only went and cut his tongue out! They reckon the quack found it in his pocket. Ha, ha, ha.'

'Jesus.' Marlowe grimaced at the thought. 'Do we know who did it?'

'If you ask me I reckon the tooth fairy got a bit carried away, he should get a few quid if he puts them under his pillow, there wasn't many left in his mouth.' Cleeves dropped his roll up to the floor, ground it out and was still laughing to himself as he went back inside and left the DCI to finish his smoke alone.

***

'Dave, got a minute?' Marlowe said sticking his head around his office door way into the main squad room. DI Dave Gowan stopped what he was doing and followed Marlowe back into his glass cubicle of an office. 'Have a seat, Dave.' Gowan folded himself into the low sofa. 'I've just been having a look at the file on John Finch.'

'Right, the bloke with his ears sliced off, what about him?' Gowan settled back in his seat.

'It says in the small print he's an associate of Chas Logan,' Marlowe said passing the file across.

'I know Logan well enough, but I'm not with you, boss?' He opened the folder and started to read, wondering where the conversation was going.

'Seems Logan was admitted into HRI yesterday afternoon,' Marlowe said then left a small pause, 'some bastard cut his tongue out.'

'Bloody hell, you are jesting?' The DCI gave him one of those raised eyebrow looks. 'I bet Trevor had something to say about that, he's such a sadistic sod.'

'And it appears he's not the only one in the city,' said the DCI as he leaned forward in his chair resting his elbows on the desk.

'Well there's one or two of them in Hull, one in particular comes to mind.'

'Mr Murphy?' Marlowe eased back in his chair.

'You've read my mind, boss.' Gowan replied as he slid the folder back across the desk.

'Yeah ok, I see your reasoning, but why would he be so callous to a couple of small fry crooks like Logan and Finch?'

'Maybe they're the blokes responsible for doing him over. Fancy a coffee?' Marlowe shook his head.

Gowan thought for a second or two. 'Why the hell would they pick on a bloke like Murphy?'

'I can't answer that, but I tell you what, Dave, if it was them it must have been something worth taking the risk for. I think another hospital visit is called for?' The team were becoming regulars at the Hull Royal Infirmary.

'Let's have another coffee before we go,' Gowan suggested.

'We, where did you get the *we* from?'

'Might have known.' Gowan strutted out of the room shouting for Jonno.

***

The traffic at the corner of the Boulevard was at a standstill, the traffic lights were on the blink again. DCs Lee Kristianson and Tanya Etherington stood staring down into the excavated hole in the pavement. 'My Gran used to live on Hessle Road,' Lee said above the din of the traffic noise.

'Whereabouts?' asked Tanya, interested.

'Dunno.'

'Is that it?' She waited for him to continue.

'Mmm.' He was miles away.

'Well that was a very informative conversation.' Tanya was mystified. 'Anyway, put this on.' She passed him a yellow hard-hat.

'You don't think I'm going down there do you?'

'If you see where the bones were found it might give you a better grasp of things.'

'But…I've got my good suit on!' Lee protested.

'Lee, you are such a girl at times, get down the hole.' Reluctantly he put on the hard-hat and climbed down the ladder. 'Oi, look the other way you perv,' Tanya yelled down the hole as she followed him down the ladder. Lee laughed as he brushed the dust from his suit.

'Well that was very enlightening,' said Lee when they ascended once more into day light. 'Thanks for that, there was bugger all to see but bricks and rubble.'

'And the tunnel.'

'Oh yes, let's not forget another hole, some tunnel.'

'What's up with you? Tanya asked. He merely shrugged in response. 'Come on, we've got some doors to knock on.'

'This is a complete waste of our time, Tanya, I reckon if there's anyone still living around here they won't remember anything, if they do it would be bugger all worth knowing.'

Tanya felt the same about things but she wasn't about to let on, this was her chance to prove herself to the boss, but she wasn't going to let her colleague know.

'Come on, let's get back to the station and see if Missing Persons have come up with anything.' Lee tried unsuccessfully to avoid the door to door enquiries.

'You forget…knocking on doors?' Tanya reminded him.

'Oh yeah, that.'

***

'Once upon a time, many moons ago, I fancied being a doctor.' Jonno said as he drove the pool car into the Hull Royal infirmary car park. 'No, I'm serious,' he said when he saw the look of surprise on his colleagues face.

'What stopped you?' Gowan asked as they walked across the car park, he couldn't help but smile at the thought.

'Things.' Jonno replied.

'What sort of *things*?' Now Gowan *was* curious.

'Personal stuff, I don't want to go into it.' Jonno quickened his step, leaving Gowan two steps behind.

'Hang on a minute, if it's personal why bloody say something in the first place? Honestly, Jonno.'

'I'm afraid of bloody needles, ok, so now you know.'

'Some doctor you'd have made!' To which they both burst out laughing.

The two detectives made their way through the throng of visitors and patients cramming the Infirmaries smoke filled entrance. Many of the patients were in their dressing gowns and connected to mobile drips and electronic monitoring equipment, but it didn't stop the determined from having a smoke.

'It defies all common sense, don't you think?' Gowan nodded his head towards a woman sat in a wheel chair with both legs amputated, smoking her head off.

'You again,' said the charge nurse as they entered ward twelve on the fourth floor.

'I thought you were in charge on ward seven?' said Gowan, surprised at seeing her.

'You know what it's like, some bugger on sick so I got moved. Anyway who have you come to arrest this time?'

'We haven't come to arrest anyone. We're not the Stazi going around arresting everybody in sight.'

'Sorry, let me re-phrase the question. Whom have you come to interrogate?'

Gowan laughed. 'Mr Chas Logan, if he's up to seeing people?'

'Ah, you do know he won't be saying anything?' she replied seriously.

'Why, has the cat got his tongue?' It took Jonno all the time not to laugh at his own joke.

'That's not very nice.' They all smiled nevertheless. Then as quick as a flash she added. 'It might have done if it hadn't been in his pocket.'

'Good one, and you tell us we're not very nice,' said Jonno.

'This way, officers.' The charge nurse led them a little way down the corridor to a small non-descript side ward and opened the door without knocking. Chas Logan lay in a semi upright position supported by pillows. His nose had spread across his face and was held together with skilful suturing and sticking plasters. The effect was complimented with big black swollen Panda eyes. Below the thing that used to be a nose, was a narrow slit between fat, swollen lips that hid the atrocity inside his mouth.

'Bloody hell, Chas, who the hell did you upset to end up in that state?' There wasn't a cat-in-hells chance of the man in the bed answering back. If he had been in a position to respond the drugs would have prevented it, he was as high as a kite. Drips were going in and tubes were coming out and machines bleeped.

'What a lovely shade of bluish purple,' Jonno said as he went for a closer look, peering into the swollen face.

'Matches the curtains, don't you think?' All the time the banter went on Logan had to lay there and take it.

'Now then you two, that's enough joking.' The nurse was all for a joke but she thought they were going a bit too far.

'Sorry,' Gowan sounded sincere, at first. 'Tho, when do you think we can thpeak with him?' For all the drugs he was on, hate still registered in Logan's eyes.

'Out Now! I won't have you upsetting my patient.' Jonno and the DI walked away laughing at the not so funny joke, to have a word with the A&E doctor who had initially treated the unfortunate Logan. The Accident and Emergency department was for once on the quiet side, the detectives made enquiries at the reception desk and were pointed towards a slim, young man wearing chinos and a short sleeved polo shirt. He had a stethoscope hanging around his neck.

'Excuse me, Doctor Carter?'

'Yes, I'm sorry you'll have to book in at the desk.' He turned to walk away.

'I'm DI Gowan and this is DC Johnson.' Carter turned around. 'Can we have a word?'

'I'm a bit busy, can you make it quick.' He made a show of looking at his watch. 'What's it about?'

'Chas Logan, the bloke who came in with his tongue in his pocket?'

'Aah I see, let's get a coffee,' he said and led them towards the bank of vending machines.'

'I thought you were busy?'

'Yes well, it's a stock answer to get rid of people I don't want to talk to.' Once they'd fed their coins, or more correctly fed Jonno's coins into the machine, they took their plastic cups of dubious looking liquid and sat on the plastic seats in the waiting area.

'What do you want to know, gentlemen?'

'Whatever you can tell us,' the DI replied.

'Which is very little. Have you seen him?' They nodded simultaneously. 'Then you know what state he's in, his nose was all but damaged beyond repair, half of the tongue was removed with what could have been a trimming knife and in the process all his front teeth were knocked out.'

'Bloody hell, it almost makes you feel sorry for him,' said the DI.

'Did he make his own way here?' asked Jonno.

Doctor Carter raised his eyebrow. 'I would have thought it impossible from what I remember.' The doctor looked at his watch.

'Won't keep you much longer. Do you know who found him?' Gowan glanced at his own wrist.

'Yes, one of the hospital security people found him outside the doors. He was propped up against the wall. That's the chap over there.' Carter pointed to a middle aged, overweight security guard wearing a stab vest, who stood with his arms crossed trying to look intimidating. And he did.

'Thank you very much for your time, Doctor Carter,' both officers shook hands with the busy medic.

'Sorry I couldn't be of more help.' Then he was off to see to the next patient.

'Got a minute?' Jonno asked the security guard.

'Problem?' he asked as he waddled across to where the detectives were sitting.

'Pull up a pew,' said Jonno.

'I'm alright standing thanks.' His attitude was one of someone who had probably had his own issues with the police in a previous life.

'You found the bloke with his tongue cut out, that right?' Jonno took out his notebook.

'Yeah that was me,' he shuffled from one foot to the other.

'Don't suppose you saw who dropped him off?' He shook his head, nodded towards the entrance doors and they followed him outside.

'He was sat down there, propped against the wall. He could have been there for half an hour for all I know.'

What about the security cameras?' Jonno glanced up and around, CCTV cameras seemed to be visible on every build corner.

'I'm sure they'll have got something, but you'll have to ask the office about that; it's nowt to do with me.'

The detectives said their thanks and let him return to his duty of standing in the corner looking threatening.

'Just had a thought, Jonno,' the DI said as they walked back to the car.

'And what would that be?'

'I was just thinking about that security bloke. That could be you when you retire from the force.'

'Sod off...sir.' They both laughed as they headed for the security office. In contrast to the staff on the ground the office team seemed quite professional and obliging, they promised to have the CCTV footage of the previous afternoon and evening sent around to the station.

The temperature had been steadily rising throughout the day with a high humidity level and the air conditioning was slow kicking in, not unusual for a well hammered police pool car. Dave Gowan opened the vehicle windows fully as they sat in a line of traffic along Anlaby Road. 'Well there's one advantage to this hot weather...' said the DI as he nodded his head in the direction of two teenage girls who may as well have been walking the streets of Hull wearing bikinis.

'Behave yourself, you're old enough to be their father,' Jonno replied as he let out the cars clutch and moved off with the slow traffic.

'One can dream, old man.' Gowan turned his head and watched as they passed the girls.

Jonno drove the pool car along Anlaby Road, turned off just before the flyover down the Boulevard and then took a right into Gordon Street, into the constricted nick car park and parked up. The first stop was the vending machine in the corridor for a couple of cold drinks. Jonno put his money in the slot and retrieved his can. 'What does that say on there? Ice cold that's what it says, this can is bloody warm.'

'Thanks for the warning, I won't bother.' Gowan headed for the water cooler. 'Mine's ice cold and free.' He taunted smugly.

'Ok then, Dave, what do you reckon is the next move?' Jonno asked as he parked his arse on the corner of the DI's desk.

'If I'm honest, Jonno, I haven't got a clue what's going on.' The DI picked up the ice cold drink and ran the cup across his forehead. 'I know we have some unsavoury sorts in our city, but this - ears cut off and tongues ripped out - in Hull, I ask you.'

'Yeah, it's a bit different to the usual good-hiding, or getting your head kicked in.'

'Tell you what though, Jonno, I'd bet your pension it's got something to do with Murphy getting done over.'

Chapter 10

Ian Anderson was one of those blokes who normally strived on a little bit of pressure, ducking, diving and living on the edge, that was his thing. But needless to say the strain of the illicit contraband they'd found in the briefcase was telling on him. He was a bag of nerves and had hardly been out of the house since that night. He'd spent the majority of the time in a semi drunken stupor, too afraid to leave the security of four brick walls and a locked door.

The case containing the stash of drugs was hidden under a pile of junk in the cupboard under the stairs. The cash had been equally shared between himself, Finch and Logan. Anderson came to the conclusion that he could not spend the rest of his miserable life hiding, it was time to bite the bullet and face the world, and after all if Murphy had been looking for him he'd have been dead by now.

He went through to the bathroom and ran himself a bath, undressed and dropped all his stinking clothes in the washing basket and climbed into the tub, in the hope that the soapy suds would wash away his troubles. He lay there in the scummy water until it went cold, shivering he dried himself off and dressed in semi-fresh clothes, picked up the whisky bottle, looked at the amber liquid swirling around and changed his mind and put the kettle on for a coffee.

The three Amigo's had gone their separate ways, it had always been the plan. Anderson had told them to keep a low profile, that was until he'd found out about Finch. The main thing was there hadn't been any further word from Mr Murphy, which could only be a good thing. Anderson thought that now might be the time to reacquaint himself with the world once more. Food was something he had been neglecting, since that night he'd settled for the solace of the bottle. Feeling a little more like his old self he realised how hungry he actually was as his stomach growled an alcohol fuelled growl. He made himself a cheese and pickle sandwich after scraping the mould off the top of the pickle. Once he'd eaten, it was going to be a trip out to his local, the *Victoria*.

Anderson thought things were definitely on the up, the birds were chirping in the trees, the sun was bright in the sky and reflecting off the drink cans on the pavement and, to top it all he had money in his pocket, a lot of money. He sucked a last drag on his tax free rollie as he approached the pub door, spat it to the pavement and walked in. The lunch time rush was over, a couple of young lads who didn't look old enough to be in the place were playing pool. At the far end of the bar a pensioner's domino school occupied one corner. No one even looked up as he entered. It was just how he liked it.

'Andy, haven't seen you for a couple of days, how you doing?' Billy the barman asked as he walked towards him from the other end of the bar, wiping down as he went.

'Not too bad, had the flu,' he lied, 'give us a pint of Best bitter.' Anderson stood leaning on the bar with one elbow and looked around.

Billy pulled a pint of Best and pushed it across the bar. 'Two fifty please, mate.'

Anderson took out a wedge of notes from his back pocket and paid with a five pound note. 'Keep the change.' Billy raised his eyebrows; it was unusual for Anderson to leave a tip. 'Chas, been in lately?' He picked up his pint and sipped through the frothy head.

'Chas, he was in lunch time day before yesterday. That nephew of Murphy's, whatcha call him? Anyway he came in looking for him.' Anderson's heart skipped a beat. 'The dickhead caused a right palaver, stuck a fork in the back of Chas' mate's hand, pinned it to the bar he did, made a right bleedin' mess of the counter top. Then Chas went off with what's his name.' Anderson put down his pint. It took him all his time to stop his hand from trembling. 'Are you alright, pal?' Billy asked with concern in his voice. 'As I was saying, I 'eard 'ees in 'ull Royal.' He picked up a rag and started to wipe down the bar top.

'Chas' mate?' Anderson asked.

'No, Chas, 'eard he's in a bad way.' He carried on wiping down, like he didn't really give a toss.

'Gimme a whisky, Billy,' he said pushing the pint further away.

'Coming up.' He paid with another five pound note. This time, to Billy's dismay his customer pocketed the change. Anderson's head was in turmoil, he hadn't banked on Murphy sussing things out so soon. He picked up the tot glass with a trembling hand and downed the whisky in one. He grimaced as the liquid burnt a path down his throat and lay like a furnace in his stomach.

'Billy, another.' Another five pound note, the barman wondered where all the money was coming from, Anderson was usually a *make a pint last half an hour* type of customer. Once again he knocked back the whisky, pushed the change across to a happy Billy and left.

It had been a nice sunny day when he'd left home, now for all the notice he took it might have been miserable and pissing down, as he trudged with his head down trying not to stand in the dog shit that littered the pavement. Once back home he headed straight for the near empty whisky bottle, to carry on where his session in the pub had been cut short. He tipped the bottle to his lips hoping to find a solution in the bottom of the bottle. He needed a plan; either that or it wouldn't be long before he ended up in the next bed to his mate Logan. He wondered what was going on with Finchy, but when he picked up his mobile and dialled Finchy's number, all he got was the "sorry cannot connect your call, please try again later". Decision made, he grabbed a bag from the bottom of the wardrobe and filled it with enough clothes and toiletries to keep him going for a few days voluntary solitary confinement. He retrieved the briefcase from the cupboard under the stairs and went out to his van. He would hide up in his sister's caravan at the east coast seaside town of Hornsea, some eighteen miles east of the city.

Chapter 11

It wasn't hard for Keane and the fat bouncer to find Anderson's ground floor flat. They waited until early evening before paying a visit. The bouncer parked the Range Rover in the communal car park around the back of Anderson's flat.

'Get your arse around the front way,' said Keane.

'Right, want me to kick the door in?' he replied over enthusiastically, there was nothing he enjoyed more than kicking things.

'Yeah, right and have all the neighbours out, leave that to me.' Keane opened the back yard gate, it wasn't locked, he walked down the path straight up to the kitchen window and stuck his face to the glass, the place looked empty. Keane returned to face the back door, he tried the door, it was locked so he took a pace backwards, swung his right leg and with a well aimed boot he politely kicked it in.

'You have a look in the bedroom, I'll check around here,' Keane wasn't optimistic in finding anything. The pair searched the flat from top to bottom. Empty, Keane knew Anderson couldn't have been gone long. It was just a feeling. A hunch. But where could he have run too? It wasn't as if Anderson had many mates, his two sidekicks were in hospital there was nowhere for him to run. But on the other hand he did have a wedge and was holding a substantial amount of a "Class A" substance, that could take him a very long way if he found a buyer brave enough to take it on.

***

Patrick Murphy self-made entrepreneur and gangster hadn't been venturing far from his home since his run in, the simple reason being he was still feeling more than a bit on the rough side. The hard man wasn't usually one for feeling sorry for himself, but today he was feeling all of his fifty eight years. He sat in his suburban home on the western edge of the city looking through the conservatory window at the paddock beyond, staring at nothing in particular. Murphy could see his drawn reflection in the plate glass and wasn't impressed. There was no two ways about it he was having a bad day. He sat with his arms wrapped around his chest nursing his broken ribs, giving the odd thought or two to what he would do to Anderson when he caught up with him, more importantly he thought of the consequences that he himself was likely to face if he didn't retrieve his goods. He still owed a substantial sum and if he didn't get his merchandise back soon he'd be in for more than a serious talking to. He may even be forced to raid his own piggy bank to pay off the debt.

Murphy heard the sound of tyres crunch on the gravel drive. He had an inkling of who it would be. Not many people would come to his home uninvited.

'You there, Uncle Pat?' Keane shouted as he came through the kitchen into the conservatory. 'How you doing?' he asked as he dropped down into an easy chair.

'Not so bad, lad.' Murphy said as he quickly withdrew his arms. He tried not to wince as he sat upright, not wanting to show any sign of weakness in front of his nephew. 'Anderson, you got him?'

'It's just a matter of time, Uncle Pat.' Keane stood, crossed to the drinks cabinet and poured two glasses of single malt, he placed one next to Murphy's bottle of pain killers on the occasional table. 'Looks like he's done a runner and gone to ground.'

'I want him found, you hear? I don't care where he is I want him and my belongings.'

'I'll ask around and get the word out.' Keane watched the old man wince.

'Do that, son.' Murphy eased back in his chair, gritted his teeth and closed his eyes.

Chapter 12

Since transferring from Driffield to Hull, Tanya had clicked with Karina the CSE and had become good friends as well as colleagues. 'So are you going to come line dancing tonight or what?' Tanya asked as they sat in the station car park soaking up the lunch time sun.

'I've already told you it's not my thing, besides I'm busy tonight,' replied the unenthusiastic CSE. She picked up her can of tepid cola and sipped.

'Doing what?' Tanya turned to face her.

'Don't know yet!' Karina stretched out her legs and raised her face to the sun.

'Come on it'll be a laugh.' Tanya tried again.

'I'd sooner watch *Top Gear* on the telly and that's saying something.' Karina could not think of anything worse than prancing around in a cowboy hat. 'How are you getting on with skelly.' Skilfully she changed the subject as she stood up and together they walked back into the office, via the water cooler in the hall. Armed with plastic cups of ice cold water they continued to the squad room.

'Slowly, nobody seems to remember much about the toilets once they'd been closed. We're still running a search on the missing person database, but it's taking time.' Tanya sat behind her desk, Karina perched on the edge.

'His clothes definitely date back to the 1970s, typical skin head type, denim jeans with the bottoms turned up, union jack tee shirt and the boots were *Doc Martins*, my guess is that they're genuine from the era.'

'Anyway, about the toilets, did I tell you about the boss and Sergeant Cleeves...' Tanya clammed up as she saw Marlowe approaching.

'You two discussing, skelly?'

'Yes, boss.'

'Well don't let me stop you.' He pulled up a chair and sat down. 'Have you had the pathology report back yet?' Marlowe asked Karina.

'Yes, we had someone from the University Anthropology Department have a look at him as well, waste of time really. He confirmed what we already knew; death was definitely due to blunt force trauma inflicted on the back of the skull.'

'For us simpletons you mean someone hit him over the head?'

'Precisely, there was a sharp corner indent through the cranium, about here.' Karina placed her hand on top of Marlowe's head, slightly towards the back.

'Nice. Any idea what the murder weapon could have been?' asked Tanya.

'Most certainly a brick, there was traces of red brick dust in the cracked bone.'

Marlowe pondered for a moment or two. 'Going back to the tunnel, how far did they get?'

'Only about three metres then they ran into trouble,' replied Karina.

'What sort of trouble?' Tanya asked as she eased forward in her chair.

'Solid Granite, I say that loosely, they ran into a wall of solid rock.'

'That can't be usual in the geology of this area surely?'

'No but if you go back a couple of hundred years to when they were building the docks, thousands of tons of rocks were used, maybe it was dumped when all the building was done.'

'Suppose it could have been, it doesn't matter or help us anyway.' Marlowe said as he shifted his cramping bottom. 'And the cave in?'

'Oh that was definitely deliberate, although short, the tunnel was well constructed with props, most were still in place. I suppose a prop or something could have given way. But it appears that the body was posed, laid in a precise position then someone went at the bricks above with a sledge hammer and down came the tunnel opening.'

'A falling out among thieves as they say. Do we know who skelly is yet?'

'Not a flippin' clue,' said Karina. 'The pathology people are doing tests on the shin bone and teeth to see if they can still find a DNA trace, we should know in a couple of days if they've been successful.'

'Then run it through the data base to see if there is a match?'

'That's the aim. Anyway we've still got a hell of a lot of debris to sift through yet, I'll let you know if anything comes up.'

'Thanks, Karina,' said the DCI.

'No probs.' Evading any more invitations from Tanya to strut her stuff, she stood up and left.

'You know where I am if you need me,' he said to Tanya and left her to it. Marlowe returned to his airless office which didn't have the luxury of being air conditioned, according to the building control people it was wasn't cost effective to install such a system in his part of the Nineteenth century building. Marlowe thought the term tight arses were more appropriate.

Chapter 13

Throughout the journey from Hull's Orchard Park Estate to Hornsea, Anderson would be the first to admit he was paranoid. His neck ached from constantly checking the rear view mirror and repeatedly looking over his shoulder through the rear screen. Deep down he knew he wasn't being followed but felt the need to be reassured all the same. Anderson headed directly for the sea front and parked the van near the promenade. He was still feeling fearful.

Once he was sure he hadn't been followed he headed for the seafront chippie, desperate for something greasy to help settle the lunchtime booze that still lay in his stomach before heading for the caravan park. With a parcel of cod and chips under his arm he found an empty bench facing the beach, and sat feeding his face whilst watching a young couple and their two children playing in the North Sea waves. While he sat he contemplated his fate, and the future wasn't looking too good from where he was sitting. Walking out into the North Sea and not turning back might be the only real solution to his dilemma.

Janice, Anderson's sister was older than him and never married. All her life she'd been careful with the pennies. With thanks to a good pension plan, she had been fortunate enough to take early retirement from her position as a secondary school head teacher. For Janice life was good, she was privileged enough to split her time between the caravan and a two bed roomed apartment in Minorca. More times than he liked to admit, Anderson thought how unfair life had been on him, she, his sister, appeared to have everything and he had nothing except a smack-head ex-wife and a council house that he struggled to pay the rent on. To be fair to his sister, she'd always been there to bail him out when things got tough, reluctantly maybe, but she always came through when she was needed.

Anderson continued to glance in the rear view mirror as he drove the van along the promenade. He turned onto the caravan park at the southern end of the sea front, past the coffee shop, children's play area and amusements. The caravan wasn't a caravan as such; it was a thirty foot long by ten foot wide luxury mobile home with two large en-suite bedrooms, deluxe fitted kitchen and lounge complete with flat screen television.

He grabbed his bag off the passenger seat, locked the van, fumbled for the caravan keys in his pocket, intermittently looking over his shoulder as he unlocked the rear side door of the luxury holiday home and went inside. As always it was spick and span with everything in its place. He dumped his bag on the floor and after a quick check that all the mains services were working he went through to the bedroom and collapsed on the bed. He lay with his hands behind his head staring up at the ceiling, wishing he'd brought a bottle of whisky with him, then he remembered he was loaded, he could afford to buy as many bottles as he wanted from the site supermarket.

***

Dave Gowan sat in his sectioned off cubicle, leaning forward resting his elbows on the surface of the desk, he gave out a big sigh and leaned back in his chair.

'Wow you meant that, something troubling you?' asked Jenny Bright as she looked over the top of the dividing section.

'Just knackered that's all,' he said as he looked up at the beaming face peering at him.

'You know the answer to that one as well as I do, an early night.' Gowan and Jenny had a good relationship, purely platonic, but if Gowan had his way things might have been different.

'Thanks for the advice, it's noted,' he smiled.

'I've been doing a bit of digging,' Jenny said as she left her side of the partition and came around to sit on the corner of the DI's desk.

'Don't tell me you've actually made a start on the garden?' he said as he sat back in his seat.

'Me gardening, you have to be kidding? No I've been looking into our Mr Murphy, it seems he's moved into loan sharking,' Jenny replied.

'Ah, that sort of digging,' he joked. 'Well I suppose it was only a matter of time, he's into everything else.'

'As far as I can make out it seems to be a legitimate business, he's recently formed a new company called *Kwik Kash.*'

'That's original for him.' Gowan smirked as he spoke.

'It's like one of these short term loan companies you see on the telly; you know who charge exorbitant interest rates. From what I can make out they are handing out cash to anyone, don't seem to carry out credit checks or anything.'

'Interesting, but what's your point?' Asked Gowan.

'Apparently John Finch took out a loan for £200 which has escalated to nearer £2500, so I'm thinking, big loan – can't pay – send in the heavies etc, I reckon we might have our link.' Jenny stood up and walked over to the open window, fanning herself with her hand. 'What do you think?'

Before the DI had a chance to reply, Sergeant Cleeves burst into the room as large as life. 'Dave, you got a minute?'

'That's all I have got, Trev,' he replied as he fastened the top button of his shirt and straightened his tie. All the time he was ready for the joke that usually followed Cleeves arrival.

'You going out?' asked Cleeves.

'I wish I was, the Super wants to see me. He wants to know what benefit I got out of the "Political Correctness Course", ha, that was a laugh a bloody minute I can tell you.'

'So you think it did you a bit of good then?' Cleeves asked with a sarcastic edge in his voice that was difficult to ignore.

'Trev, if you've just come in here to take the piss, you can bloody well bugger off again!'

Cleeves loved winding DI Gowan up, it was so easy. 'I nearly forgot what I wanted to see you about, John Finch, the bloke who misplaced his ears...' he couldn't help chuckling at his own joke.

'We've just been talking about him,' said Jenny.

Gowan stood, crossed to one of the large plate glass partitions and checked his appearance. 'What about him?'

'One of the nurses rang from HRI and said he wants to have a word with someone in CID.'

'Fantastic.' He slackened off his tie and unfastened the shirt button again. 'I'll go myself. Fancy a ride out, Jenny?'

'What about your meeting with the Super?' Jenny questioned.

'It'll keep, he's probably forgotten about it anyway.' Gowan knew that missing the meeting would result in yet another bollocking.

'If you say so, Dave, if you say so.' Cleeves replied touching the side of his nose as he left.

Jenny grabbed her shoulder bag and followed Gowan to the car park. 'Whose car are we going in, yours or mine?' The DI gave her a sideways glance. 'Looks like mine then,' she said, fishing for her keys in her bag.

Gowan wished they'd taken his Audi, as he sat in the front passenger seat of Jenny's Golf with his knees pressing against the dashboard. The tower block of the hospital loomed down on them as they pulled up in the Hull Royal Infirmary car park.

'I'm sick of coming to this place,' Gowan said as they walked across the car park and entered HRI. 'Floor twelve if I remember rightly.' He led the way to the super fast lift.

They both showed their identification to the nurse behind the nurse's station. 'You've come to see Mr Finch I presume?'

'Correct, got it in one. Is he in the same room?' She nodded. 'Thanks.'

The DI knocked on the door of the side ward and they walked into the plain drab room, this time there were no machines bleeping and humming, just its single occupant. 'You're looking a bit better than the last time I saw you,' the DI said to Finch who was fully dressed sitting in the bedside chair. He did look better, but with bandages wrapped around his head and strips of tape holding the cuts on his face together he looked like a casualty from the American Civil War.

'Discharging me in a bit,' Finch replied. He looked far from ready to be discharged. 'Just waiting for our lass to come and pick me up.'

'This is DS Bright,' said Dave as he pulled across a tubular framed chair and sat down. Jenny remained standing. 'You wanted to see us, what made you change your mind?'

'What? You'll have to shout up a bit. I have just had me ears lobbed off you know.'

'I said you wanted to see us, what made you change your mind?' Gowan shouted out, trying not to laugh.

'I didn't change my mind. If you haven't noticed I haven't been in any condition to talk to anybody, I've been drugged up to the eye balls.'

'Fair enough, what do you want to tell us?' Jenny decided to sit, took out her note book and sat ready to record the conversation. 'So...?' Gowan left the question hanging waiting for a response.

'I was - am in a bit of debt to Patrick Murphy, you know the...'

'Yes, we know who Murphy is. Is he the one who did this to you?'

'Not personally, it was that nephew of his Sean. He was the bastard with the knife.' He went visibly pale at the recollection of it as he spoke. 'That fat bouncer who works for them just grabbed my head and, well you know the rest. The doctor said they might have been able to stitch them back on if some bastard hadn't done the River Dance on them.' Jenny felt her stomach turn at the thought.

'And they did this because you owed them money?' the DI thought this was going a bit too far for an unpaid debt, even for the Murphy clan.

'Not exactly.'

'What do you mean, "not exactly"? Jenny asked, looking up from her notebook.

'I mean, yeah, I did borrow a bit of money from him, two hundred quid. I was having a bit of bother paying it back. Do you know what interest rates that bleedin' company of his charges?' he didn't wait for a reply. 'No I don't either but its fucking crippling, they reckon I owe 'em nearer two grand plus! Pass me a glass of water will you, love?' Jenny, surprised at the request, did as she was asked. 'Thanks, love.' He took the glass and gulped the tepid liquid down. 'Anyway I got a visit from the fucking nephew didn't I, Keane gave me a month to get the money in full or they'd break my bleedin' legs.

'I take it you didn't get the money?' Dave pointed to Finch's bandages.

'No, that's not what all this is about, well, not *that* money.' Dave and Jenny could guess the way the conversation was going. 'Me and a couple of mates came up with a plan of how we could get some cash.' *A plan that went drastically wrong,* thought Jenny. Logan seemed to lose concentration a little, but then again who could blame him in the circumstances.

'Finchy…you were saying,' Dave shouted, jolting him back to reality.

'Oh yeah, me and my mates thought we'd get a bit of money out of Murphy, after all he's had plenty of ours over the years.'

'It was you?'

'You mean done im over?' he nodded. 'That was us.'

Dave Gowan leaned across and offered an outstretched hand to shake Finch's. 'This is unofficial, but on behalf of all Hull coppers past and present, thanks.' A broad beaming smile appeared across Finch's face.

'The only reason I'm telling you this is cos I reckon he's after me mates.'

'Would one of those mates be called Logan?' Jenny asked.

'Chas, hell fire they got im then, is it bad?'

'I can't tell you too much, confidentiality and all that, but let's say it's bad and he won't be speaking to us - maybe when he's learned a bit of sign language.'

'Christ! Have they got hold of Andy as well?' He was starting to get into a panicky state.

'Andy who?'

'Ian Anderson, he's the other bloke who was with us when we done im.'

'You'd better tell us where we can find your mate Andy, its best we get to him first before Murphy's lot do.'

Finch reluctantly grassed on his mate, he thought it better the police get him after all it was his for his own protection and it wasn't as if Murphy would be pressing charges.

'We'll need you to come down to the station as soon as you can to make a formal statement.'

'As if that's going to happen. I can manage without me ears but my legs are a different kettle of fish.' Finch smiled for the first time.

'If you're not going to put this on record what are we doing here?' Dave was slightly pissed off. Then again it wasn't what he was expecting.

'Don't get stroppy, Mr Gowan. When we nicked the case it wasn't only cash that was in there, there was a bundle of Heroin. I reckon once you've got your hands on the drugs you'll have Murphy, his prints must be all over it.'

'Where is it now?'

'Andy's got it.'

'Where can we find this, Andy,' asked Jenny.

'E's got a flat on Orchard Park.' Jenny wrote down the address.

'Well you know where we are if you change your mind.' Dave and Jenny stood to leave, thanked him, gave him a nod and left Finch waiting for his lift home.

'What do you reckon to that?' Jenny asked.

'Well you can't blame him for not wanting to make a statement, can you image if we couldn't get the case to court his life wouldn't be worth living, never mind his legs. We'll go back to the nick and let the boss know the state of play, then I think we'll go and see if we can pick this Anderson up.'

***

'Which interview room have they put them in?' Marlowe asked Jonno.

'Number three.'

'Bloody hell, it stinks in there.' For some unfathomable reason, Building Services had never been able to find the cause of the permanent smell of sewers.

'That's ok, he's a piece of shit anyway he should feel right at home.' Marlowe didn't reply, just raised his eyebrows.

'Is there any special way you want to do this?'

'No point trying to do anything fancy, Jonno, you know as well as I do he's been in the game too long.'

'Ready then?'

'Finish my tea first,' Marlowe replied and picked up his Hull City mug.

As soon as the door to interview room number three was opened a heavily deodorised smell attacked their nostrils. The club owner sat at the interview table beside his lawyer. His face still swollen from the beating was shades of blues and purple, his arm was still supported in a sling across his chest. Murphy's brief looked expensive, everything he was wearing looked handmade, even his face looked like stretched plastic, as if it had been rebuilt more than once.

'DCI Marlowe, have you met my legal representative Mr Alan Brigham?' Murphy said as they entered the room. Marlowe ignored the club owner and sat down at the Formica topped table. DC Johnson pulled out the remaining chair and sat beside the DCI. 'Must be a bit deaf, probably his age,' said Murphy as he looked to his lawyer shrugging his shoulders.

Jonno took two brand new blank tape cassettes off the table and proceeded to remove the cellophane covering, while Marlowe carried out his predictable pretence of reading through the case file before him. Brigham appeared far from happy with the proceedings. He'd been kept waiting for half an hour before the officers had made an appearance.

'Detective Chief Inspector, are we to be kept waiting much longer? This duress is putting strain upon my client, whom I'm sure you are aware is currently not in the best of health.' Marlowe lifted his head from the folder and looked over the top of his reading glasses at the lawyer. He'd never seen such an obvious tuck and lift job, he wondered if the tight facial skin was tied in a bow at the back of his neck. He smiled. 'I insist we proceed with this interview immediately, or as my client is not under arrest I will terminate this charade forthwith.' Marlowe wondered how he could speak through the tight lips of a mouth that didn't appear to open and close.

Marlowe let the silence continue a little longer while Jonno finished putting the cassettes into the machine. Jonno gave him the nod and stated who was in the room, '...for the benefit of the tape...' Once Jonno had finished his spiel the DCI took off his reading glasses and carefully placed them on the table. He leaned forward and rested on his elbows.

'Mr Brigham, your client is here voluntarily and he is free to leave whenever he chooses, however, as you well know we look favourably on him freely participating in this interview.' This time it was Brigham who raised his eyebrows. 'Mr Murphy, we've been investigating two very serious assaults...'

'And who the feck am I supposed to have assaulted?' His lawyer leaned and whispered in his ear, Murphy shook his head.

'Did I say you had assaulted anyone? Mr Murphy, you're putting words in my mouth.' Marlowe allowed himself a smile, he had touched a nerve.

'As I was saying during the course of our investigations your name has been brought to our attention.' Again the whispering between the lawyer and client. 'I take it you do know Mr Chas Logan and Mr John Finch?'

'Never feckin heard of them.' The large frame of the club owner looked very uncomfortable perched on the plastic moulded chair.

'Funny our information tells a different story,' said Jonno.

'And who pulled your chain, son?' Murphy threw back at him. Brigham moved in close, obviously telling his client to keep things civilised. 'Well your information is feckin wrong, ok? I'm telling you I've never heard of them.'

'And I don't suppose if we do an audit of the books at Kwik Kash we won't find a record of Mr Logan borrowing from the company?' Marlowe threatened.

'You might do, you might not. I wouldn't have a clue. I'm not involved in the day to day running of the business. Do you know how many companies I run? No? I can tell you it's too many for me to know the ins and outs of all of them.'

'And your nightclub, do you take much interest in that?'

'No more than the other businesses, I leave that to my nephew. That's not to say I don't show my face on occasions. Have you been to my club?' He looked from one officer to the other. 'If you want I'll have you put on the VIP list for this weekend.'

'Thanks very much for the offer but I think we'll have to decline.' The offer did give Marlowe the idea of sending in a couple of younger officers to check the place out when the activity was in full swing, and he had just the pair in mind.

'Chief Inspector, this conversation is getting us nowhere, if there are no further question…' Brigham was already packing away paperwork into his brief case as he spoke.

'No, that will be all, gentlemen…for now.' Marlowe remained seated as Brigham stood and left the room. It was obvious Murphy was still in some pain.

'He's not an easy bloke to read is he?' said the DI.

'He's been around the block more than a few times; he knows the ropes as well as we do,' Marlowe replied as he stood up. 'Let's grab a coffee then I'll sort out a warrant, I think it's about time we went and had a look at Murphy's night spot.'

***

'Tanya!' DS Jenny Bright called out when she saw the DC disappear around the corner into the CAD Room.

'What can I do for you, sarge?' Tanya asked as she did an about-turn.

'I was wondering how things are going with the toilet-man. Let's grab a cold drink and you can bring me up to date.'

'Toilet-man? Oh sorry, didn't get it at first, you mean skelly. We still haven't managed to get an ID yet,' she said as she reached into the canteen drinks cooler.

'How about DNA?'

'Still a long way from getting any results, we're not on the priority list.'

'Understandable I suppose in the circumstances, never mind a "cold case" it's almost freezing. What have you got Lee on with?'

'He's liaising with *MISPER*, the last time I saw him he was searching through a heap of files that never found their way into the computer system. I know it's a long shot but we've got an approximate date of when we assume it all happened, and I'm thinking if he was a local bloke someone might have reported him missing.'

'At least it'll keep him occupied and you know where he is.'

'Oh he's not so bad, just got a low attention threshold.'

'If you say so, just keep him busy. Have the Crime Scene team found anything useful?'

'They're still sorting through it all. They must have shifted two tons of rubble and muck.'

'Ok, keep me in the loop, you know where I am if you want anything.'

'Cheers, sarge.'

Chapter 14

Anderson had begun to think that maybe, just maybe he'd gotten away with it. He'd been at the caravan park for two days and there had been no sign of Murphy's henchmen. Keeping on the cautious side he'd never left the caravan in daylight hours, except to buy his whisky that is, and even then he'd never gone further than the park mini market. Feeling sorry for himself he sat glass in hand, staring at the muted television screen. He was roused from his daze by the sound a heavy vehicle crunching along the caravan park's gravel road.

Keane pulled the 4x4 into the side of the gravel road beside the mobile home. For a while he and the fat bouncer sat and watched, looking for a twitch in the curtains before making their approach.

Anderson moved the net curtain aside and peered through the glass. That's when the panic set in. 'Shit, shit, shit,' he said under his breath as he dropped the curtain back into place and moved on unsteady legs away from the window. Catching the opened bottle of whisky with his elbow, he it sent it crashing to the floor. Anderson was in no doubt about the black 4x4 pulling up on the grass verge; it belonged to the Murphy clan. He put the glass on the coffee table and stood in the middle of the floor hugging his arms around himself, *where can you hide in a fucking caravan?*, he questioned himself as he dropped down on all fours and crawled the full length of the mobile home to the end bedroom.

'I tell you he's in there, I can't hear anything but I can smell the whisky from out here,' said the fat bouncer with his ear pressed up against the side of the caravan.

'Don't be stupid,' Keane snapped.

'I'm telling you, Sean, since the last time my nose was broke it's become real sensitive, the bastard is in there I'm telling you.'

'Move out of the way.' Keane shoved the bouncer aside and hammered on the caravan's aluminium panels. 'If you're in there and you don't come out and face the fucking music now, you little shit, I'll burn you out.' He kept his voice reasonably low, he didn't want the neighbours calling the police.

The mobile home shook on its base as the men outside hammered with their fists on the outer skin, Anderson heard the voices and the dread set in even further as he anticipated his fate. Still on his hands and knees he struggled to keep his wits about him, he knew what Keane was capable of and he didn't want to die, not yet anyway. The trouble was trying to conceal anything, let alone himself, in a mobile home is an impossible thing to do. There was no room under the bed for dust never mind a full grown man, and the narrow wardrobe was not an option. Almost slithering on his stomach like a snake, Anderson opened the shower cubicle door and crawled into the small booth and curled himself into the foetal position.

'Bet you didn't know I worked in caravans for a bit did you?' said the bouncer.

'And what's that got to do with the price of fish?' Keane demanded to know.

'I know how we can get in without smashing the door.'

'Why the fuck didn't you say so before.'

The bouncer shrugged. 'Have you got your carpet knife with you?' Keane put his hand into his pocket and produced the knife, the same one used to remove Finch's ears...and Logan's tongue.

'Give it here.' Keane did as he was asked. 'Just keep an eye out.' The bouncer took the knife, slipped out the sharp blade and walked around the blind-side of the mobile home, away from view.

Scratch, scraaatch, scraaatch. Anderson listened to the noise against the side of the caravan, he didn't know what it was but he *did* know it wasn't good. He tried to take some conciliation in the fact that the drugs were stashed away, safe he hoped, as long as he had what they wanted he knew he was still in with a chance of keeping his life.

'How's it going?' Keane asked poking his head around the corner of the mobile home.

'Two minutes, nearly there.' The bouncer continued scoring the trimming knife blade across the reasonably soft aluminium panel. He'd already sliced through two sides of a rectangular opening and was working on the top edge. 'Done.' The bouncer grabbed the top of the flapping panel, holding it firmly with two hands he tore the aluminium downward and revealed a gaping hole. 'Whala!'

'Now what?' The fat bouncer stood back from the hole, swung his right leg back and then forward and proceeded to kick in the mobile home's interior panel until there was a hole large enough for a man to scramble through.

Inside the shower cubicle Anderson could hear the boot connecting with the thin plywood, he prayed that someone would disturb them, that they'd go and leave him alone. He knew there was zero chance of that happening and continued trying to disappear through the shower tray base.

'Well in you go,' Keane gestured to the opening with an outstretched arm.

'Come off it, mate, I can't get a leg in there, never mind my arse.'

'You would if you weren't so fucking fat! Give me a hand.' Keane stuck his arms forward into the opening, followed by his head and shoulders. The bouncer wasn't going to waste the opportunity and gave a hefty push. 'Steady you fucking idiot, it looks like I'm getting into a box or something.'

'Come on, Sean, how was I to know, you'd end up in one of the lounge seats, just push upwards with your shoulders and the cushion will come off.' The bouncer inwardly laughed at the situation.

'I'll give you *lounge seat* when I fucking come out,' Keane wriggle the rest of his body inside the confined space. Once he'd managed to manoeuvre himself into the kneeling position, he raised himself on all fours and pushed up with his back. Sure enough whatever was above him gave way, a plywood board topped with a deep cushion sprang off enabling Keane to stand up. Keane had to hand it to his fat mate, he'd got this one right, but he'd never tell him. He walked across the lounge and unlocked the front door.

'Nice,' said the bouncer as he walked in and looked around, 'very nice.' Keane put his finger to his lips gesturing for the fat man to keep quiet. He stood stock still for a minute or two, no sound could be heard.

Keane smiled. 'Annndddyyy, Andy Andy Andy, come out, come out wherever you are,' Keane called out in childish sing song voice. 'Where are you, Andy?' Then the tone of his voice changed to one of menace. 'Come out now you fucker, 'cos I'll swing for you if I have to search for you,' nothing just silence.

Anderson, squashed tight in the shower, could hear his own heart beating; he hope Keane couldn't hear the thud, thud coming out of his chest.

'Ok, you've had your chance.' Together Keane and the bouncer started to systematically wreck the place just for the hell of it. Cupboard doors were ripped off, seats pulled to pieces and fittings torn off the wall, room by room they continued until they reached the bedroom, there was no place left to hide.

Keane stood in the bedroom doorway, there was no other place of concealment left. 'My patience is wearing very thin, you'd better get your arse out here now.' Keane took two small steps into the bedroom, pulled the duvet off the bed and threw it to the floor then pulled the wardrobe doors of their hinges, slowly he turned to face the only place left, the built in shower cubicle. Smiling to himself he slid open the circular moulded door. 'There you are Andy, been looking all over for you.' Anderson cowered in the base of the cubicle. 'Come on, out you come.' He reached in with one hand, grabbed Anderson by the hair, yanked him out and threw him to the floor. 'Now then Andy, you led us on a right dance, we've been searching all over fucking Hull for you,' he looked to his companion, 'give him his present.'

'Urgh,' groaned Anderson as the bouncers boot connected with his ribs knocking all the breath out of his body, he circled his arms around his head in self preservation for the anticipated head kick. It didn't come, but he did feel and hear his own ribs crack when the boot connected again.

Keane knelt down on the floor close to the curled up man, pulled Anderson's wrapped arms away from his head and moved in close. 'We're not here for the sea air, now where it is?' Another kick to the ribs. 'Where is it?'

'I…I don't know…can't remember,' Anderson said between sobs.

'Well which one is it? Don't know or can't remember? 'cos you're the only fucker that does know?' Keane spat out.

'Arggh,' Anderson screamed out loud as the bouncer grabbed him by the ankles and dragged him roughly from the bedroom to the lounge and the boot connected once again, this time dead-legging his thigh muscle.

Anderson lay at Keane's feet clutching his broken body. From the pain he was feeling he thought maybe more than one rib had been broken.

'It doesn't look like it's here or we'd have found it,' Keane said looking around at the destruction they'd brought about.' He picked up Anderson's tumbler of whisky and held it to the light. Wiping away the smears from around the rim he then knocked back the cheap fiery liquid in one. 'Let's get back, put him in the car.' He threw the glass into the flat screen television and walked outside.

All Anderson could think of was what his sister was going to say about her wrecked home, she'd probably kill him.

The bouncer opened the rear door of the Range Rover and threw Anderson onto the back seat, cracking his head on the door frame along the way.

'Oh no, you dirty bastard,' Keane shouted as Anderson lost control of his bowels. 'Why did you think we didn't beat your face to a pulp? 'Cos I didn't want your claret all over the bleedin' upholstery, that's fucking why, and now what have you gone and done but shit yourself you dirty little fucker. Get the mongrel out and shove him in the boot.'

Chapter 15

'So, where did you find Anderson's ex-wife?' asked the DCI as he approached Tanya's desk.

'It wasn't easy I can tell you,' replied Tanya who was fighting a losing battle with the plastic wrapping on her pre-packed sandwich. 'Why do they have to make these so bloody difficult?' Holding the plastic between her teeth she ripped the wrapper wide nearly spilling the contents across the desk.

'It's never easy with piss-heads and junkies, never where you expect them to be. When you do find them they're either drunk or stoned and it takes a month of Sundays to get any sense out of them.'

'We trailed all over the city checking the homeless hostels, any place where we thought she might be hanging out but nobody had seen her in days. It was one of Jonno's snouts who gave us the heads up where to find her. Turned out she was dossing down in a manky squat, back of a closed down shop along Anlaby Road. What a bloody dump, no running water, toilets clogged up, not flushing and shi..'

'Ok, steady up, Tanya, I've just had my lunch.'

Tanya smiled and took a bite of her own lunch and carried on. 'Talk about a mess, and I'm talking about her now. The state of her, all skin and bone with a face full of scabs, looked like she hadn't had a good dinner in weeks. Jonno reckoned she was turning tricks to keep alive. God knows who'd pay good money to go with her.'

'Takes all sorts, it's surprising what blokes will pay for when they've had a skinful.'

'Anyway, it turns out his sister is worth a bob or two. She lives the best part of the year in the sunshine, Menorca, Majorca or somewhere, but she keeps a posh caravan at Hornsea for the few months a year when she comes home. That cost me a tenner by the way.' The last comment washed straight over the DCI.

Marlowe stood quiet, thinking. Tanya could almost see the cogs working in his head. 'Right, I'm going for a fag. Have a word with Trev and get a couple of uniforms sorted and we'll take a trip out to the seaside. Let's just hope we find Anderson before Murphy gets his hands on him.'

It was an exceptionally busy day for the city's police force. There couldn't have been a worse time to request uniform back-up. Officers had been seconded from all sub-stations in the area, to oversee an unofficial protest march through the city centre by Council employees, protesting over cuts to pension and redundancy payments. Sergeant Cleeves stood resting on his elbows on the high level desk, writing in the duty log as Tanya approached and made her request.

'Tanya, no, I haven't got any spare bods for a jaunt out to the coast.' Cleeves said shaking his head without even looking up.

'Come on, sarge, don't be like that, the DCI said…'

Cleeves looked up. 'I don't care what the PI said or didn't say, I can't spare anyone. You go back and tell him…' he abruptly stopped as two constables walked in through the back door. 'You two, what are you on with?'

'Just going on our rest break, sarge,' the lead officer said as they tried to make off to the canteen.'

'Rest break my arse, you've only been on duty an hour and a half. You're going to the seaside. DC Etherington, two of my finest officers for the use of.'

'But, sarge…' the uniform tried again.

'Stop whinging, the Detective Constable will brief you.' Cleeves put his head down to carry on with the log. 'Grab yourselves a quick brew, and I mean quick,' he added before they could protest further.

Just my luck thought Tanya. The two officers to accompany her and the DCI were her least favourite pair of uniformed officers in the city, never mind station. There weren't any worse sexist, homophobic bigots and piss-takers anywhere. In the circumstances she supposed they were better than no-one, but only just.

The patrol car took the lead out of the city on the sixteen mile journey to the coast. Tanya and Jonno followed in Marlowe's Mondeo, with the DCI driving. 'Brought a towel and your cozzie with you, Jonno?' asked Marlowe.

'If only you'd mentioned it earlier, sir.' Jonno replied, glancing to Tanya and rolling his eyes.

'Saw that,' said Marlowe smiling into the rear view mirror. 'You could always go in the buff.'

'Yeah right, if only I had a towel.' It was evident to Tanya that Marlowe and Jonno had been friends and colleagues for a long time.

'Never mind, Jonno, the boss might buy us an ice cream,' said Tanya joining in the banter.

The seaside town of Hornsea was once a thriving place until the Beacham railway cuts of the early 1960s. Now the resort really struggled to hold its own and survive against the larger resort of Bridlington just a few miles further up the coast.

Nevertheless, the day was busy with holiday makers and day trippers visiting the beach and the Hornsea Freeport shopping complex. The traffic crawled through the small town centre, the police vehicles followed suit keeping pace with the traffic, not wanting to cause alarm or panic amongst the holiday makers. A discreet approach was the order of the day with the patrol car refraining from using sirens on Marlowe's instruction. Considering how busy the seaside resort was, the South Beach Caravan Park was extremely quiet. Marlowe concluded that most people were taking advantage of the fine sunny day on the beach.

The two vehicles slowed and pulled up along the promenade, the caravan park entrance was just up ahead, a hundred metres or so. The uniformed officers left their vehicle and approached the Mondeo for instructions.

'If Anderson is in there he's going to be scared, so let's do this quietly. Tanya you're less scary looking out of all of us,' she blushed, 'just walk straight up to the door and give it a knock. And you two,' he said to the uniforms, 'start making your way around the other side, you never know he might try and make his escape through a window. Right let's go.'

The small task force went the rest of the way on foot. The mobile home stood in a prime location, with perfect views over the North Sea. Marlowe stood back whilst Tanya cautiously approached the mobile home; she was just about to knock on the glass panel door and stopped arm mid-stretch. 'Sir, you'd better come and have a look at this,' a voice sounded out from around the blindside of the mobile home.

'I thought I told you to keep bloody quiet until we know if he's in there or not!'

'My guess is NOT...SIR, there's a bloody great gaping hole through the side of the caravan, SIR.' The attitude was well noted by the DCI.

With caution put aside, Marlowe approached the mobile home. 'Bloody hell,' the aluminium panel was flapping in the breeze. 'Don't touch it we might get some prints off it.' the PC with attitude stepped away. Marlowe walked back around the other side of the mobile home, pulled a pair of latex gloves from his pocket and stretched them over his hands. Carefully he opened the door and went inside followed by Tanya and Jonno, the uniformed officers remained outside.

'What a bloody shambles,' Jonno said as he looked around at the debris.

'Well it definitely wasn't a visit by the tidy police.' Tanya commented.

Marlowe wrinkled his nose at the smell of booze. 'Leave the door open and let some fresh air in or we'll all end up pissed.' Carefully he picked up the whisky glass and held it to the light. 'Looks like we'll get some decent prints anyway,' he put the glass back down. 'Give the lads outside a hand knocking on a few doors, see if the neighbours saw or heard anything. You never know we might get lucky.' The DCI thought this was highly unlikely on such a fine sunny day. Most people were at the beach sunning themselves or meandering around the shops.

'Tanya, get on the blower and arrange for a Crime Scene team to get down here, I want the place given a thorough going over, inside and out. Then you and me will have a look around.' He turned on the spot taking in the mayhem. 'From the state of the place I don't suppose we'll find anything.' Marlowe thought it was the story of his life, always too late for the party. Carefully, disturbing as little as possible they carried out a superficial search. As expected as far as finding anything that could be used as evidence, the search turned out to be next to useless. It had been wishful thinking on his part that they would strike it lucky and find the drugs concealed in the mobile home. Marlowe could only pin his hopes that the CSE team would have better luck.

'No joy with any of the neighbours,' said Jonno as he returned from knocking on doors. 'Most of them are out having donkey rides on the beach or eating fish and chips.'

'Thought as much.' He turned to face the uniformed officer without the attitude. 'I want you to stay on the scene until the Crime Scene bods arrive. You,' he said sharply to the other, 'can come back with us.'

***

The heat in the squad room hung heavy, the open windows did little to help circulate the stale air. DI Gowan sat behind his desk, shirt sleeves rolled up, top button undone and his tie hung loose around his neck. He took out his handkerchief and wiped it across his forehead.

'Have you got a minute, sir?' DC Kristianson asked as he ran his finger around the inside of his shirt collar, his other arm wrapped around a bundle of buff coloured folders.

'Lee, you are allowed to undo the top button of your shirt you know.'

Kristianson didn't need telling twice, he put down the files and unfastened the top shirt button and loosened his tie.

'Right, now what can I do for you?'

'You know I'm working with Tanya on the skeleton case?' He hovered from left foot to right and back again.

'Yeah right, having problems?'

'No, no problems. I've been trailing through the MISPER reports from 1978 and I think I might have turned something up.'

Gowan pushed back his chair and stood up to open window hoping to catch the nonexistent breeze. 'Go on, I'm listening.'

'Well, a young bloke was reported missing in July of that year and by all accounts the description given at the time *could* match our skelly.'

'Could? What was the description, a very thin bloke and in need of a hot dinner?' Gowan joked.

'You know what I mean sir, mid twenties, wearing skinhead clothing, approximately the same height forensics reckon our bones would have been.'

'It seems that trawl through the old records might have paid off then, good work.' Lee's face lit up at the compliment, Gowan was always quick to take the piss out of the youngster and not so quick when praise was needed. The young DC was like the cat that got the cream.

'Who reported him missing?' Gowan asked.

'His wife.'

'Wife…you've got her name and contact details?'

'Yeah, but it was years ago she probably won't be living at the same address.' Lee replied as he checked the file. 'Shall I go around and see if she's still there?'

'No, don't go jumping your guns, remember you're not working the case alone, it's all about teamwork. Wait until you've brought Tanya up to speed, then you can do the follow up. In a case as old as this it will be very difficult to prove he's the missing husband. It will all probably boil down to DNA. You never know you might fall lucky if she kept any of his belongings. Ok?'

'Thanks for that, sir.'

'Let me know how you get on.'

Chapter 16

'Open the bloody windows, it's starting to stink in here.' The vehicles air-conditioning had difficulty coping with the smell coming from the rear of the range Rover.

Keane and the fat bouncer had just passed through the village of Leven, when Keane's mobile rang. 'No prizes for guessing who this is,' Keane said as he pressed the accept key.

'Where are you?' Patrick Murphy said into his phone.

'Just coming into the city,' replied the nephew.

'You got the fecker?'

'Oh yes,' he replied as he glanced over his shoulder to the luggage area of the Range Rover where Anderson cowered in his own filth. 'He sends his regards. See you at the club then.' The line went quiet. 'You still there, Uncle Pat?'

'Yeah, I'm still here. No not the club, bring him around here.'

'The house, you must be joking?' Keane looked to the bouncer and raised his eyebrows.

'Deadly serious, when you get here take him straight to the stables.' He hung up leaving Keane wondering what on earth his uncle was playing at.

***

The day had been a long one. Marlowe, who lived for the job, was ready for home long before finishing time, which was unusual for him. Although he enjoyed spending time in the galley of the Daisy he was not in the mood for cooking and a take-away from the *All Electric Fisheries* on the Beverley road beckoned him. A paper parcel comprising of an extra large Haddock and chips, complete with mushy peas accompanied him for the rest of the journey home. 'Come on, come on, my tea's getting cold,' he cursed as he crawled along in the stream of slow moving traffic.

Archie knew the sound of the Mondeo's rough engine, long before the vehicle came into view and was there to greet him as he entered the secure compound. With the dog trotting by his side they clambered aboard the *Daisy*. In the tiny self-contained galley with his evening meal warming up in the microwave, he poured himself a glass of Spanish Rioca. He sipped and savoured as he waited for the ping to tell him the meal was ready. A decision was made to dine alfresco on the aft deck. The evening still retained enough warmth to warrant Marlowe lingering on the *Daisy's* deck with another glass of Rioca, long after his meal was finished.

'Hey up, lad,' a voice called out of the darkness, startling Marlowe as his eyes closed and his head started to droop. 'Fancy coming for a pint?' It was Harry from the Old Lock Keepers Cottage.

'Very tempting, but not tonight, mate if you don't mind. I'm just about done in, ready for my bed.'

'Another time then. Goodnight, son.' Marlowe watched the old man limp his way along the tow-path heading for the *Sloop*. Marlowe smoked a last cigarette before bed as Archie sniffed around along the tow-path.

Chapter 17

It had been two days since Andy Anderson had been invited to enjoy the hospitality of Patrick Murphy's luxurious home. The detached country villa was a far cry away from his ex-council house. Not that Anderson had been invited to enjoy the comforts of the five bedrooms, the snooker room or the indoor swimming pool. But enjoyment was not on the agenda Murphy proposed. At the bottom of the long gravel driveway which led to the paddock, was a purpose built log and timber stable block that housed Murphy's niece's ponies, usually. Now the ponies had a house guest, Anderson.

By horsey standards the place was of first class accommodation, but lacking in any luxury fixtures and fittings that a human would enjoy. Despite the heat outside and even greater heat inside, the stable windows remained permanently shut and the smell inside the timber building was building to the vomiting stage. It wasn't the ponies that were responsible for the stench, but Anderson. A sound barrier had been constructed from bales of hay and straw in the centre of the stable. Excrement, urine and blood pooled on the concrete floor.

A thin plume of blue smoke rose and spiralled into the air from Murphy's miniature cigar. 'Doing well isn't he?' he said, pointing the cigar in Keanes' direction. 'A skinny fella like him, I thought he would have been feckin dead by now. You wouldn't have lasted this long, lad,' he said to his nephew. Anderson, naked except for his dirty stained underpants slumped almost semi-comatose on a bale of hay, his ankles firmly tied together, his hands, behind his back were tied at the wrist with coarse rope. The end of the rope was fixed to a pulley wheel suspended from a sturdy timber roof beam. 'Let's have him up.'

The fat bouncer, who had been standing to one side of the proceedings feeding his face with a sausage roll, stuffed it in his mouth and crossed to where the rope was fixed. He untied the slack rope from around the cleat and took the weight. In one big heave he began to pull into the air. The broken body groaned as loud as his bloody mouth would allow as he was hoisted off the ground. With his arms stretched outward and upward behind his back, Anderson thought for sure his shoulders would be dislocated this time.

The pain inflicted on him during his incarceration had been unbearable. He didn't know how much more punishment he could take, he'd already told them all he knew. He thought he would have been released a life time ago, now he knew that was never going to happen, it had never been a part of Murphy's plan. Hoisted with his arms taking the full weight of his body, his black and blue beaten legs could no longer support his weight. He hung there like a rag doll. He'd given up trying to look defiant, he lifted his head slightly and squinted through swollen eyes looking for pity that would never come.

'I'll say this for you fella, for a little shite you've got some balls and I mean that as a complement. And talking about balls...' Murphy looked towards his nephew. Keane who had been standing to one side of the proceedings, put his cigarette between his lips and came forward. Looking directly into the swollen slits that were once Anderson's eyes, he smiled. He continued to watch the battered face as he pulled Anderson's disgusting underpants down around his ankles. Murphy shouldered his nephew out of the way and looked the stricken man in the face, then stubbed out his cigar in Andersons groin. Limp, beaten and degraded Anderson could not only feel the flesh burning, he could smell it, and for third time that day he passed out.

'Smells like a piece of pork steak cooking,' the fat bouncer said. No one answered.

'What do you reckon now, Uncle Pat?'

Murphy picked up a piece of Anderson's discarded clothing and wiped his sweaty palms. 'What do I reckon? I'll tell you what I reckon, son. I'm going for a cup of tea and to get my head down for an hour or two. You two can get your arses back to Hornsea and get the merchandise, then we'll finish what we've started.'

To be on the safe side of things, not wanting any unwanted screams to escape from the barn, Murphy stuffed the dirty rag he'd wiped his hands with in the mouth of the unconscious man. The bouncer let go of the rope and Anderson fell to the concrete floor in a crumpled heap. Just for good measure Keane stuck the boot in and spat on the broken bundle.

***

'Knock, knock,' said Karina the Chief CSE as she peered around Marlowe's open door, got a minute?'

'Depends,' Marlowe inclined his head to the growing pile of paperwork that was taking over his desk.

'Thought you might like to see this.' She produced a heavy looking evidence bag she'd been concealing behind her back, and slapped it down hard on the desk.

'That what I hope it is?' Marlowe sat forward and picked up the bag, a 2kilo package of Heroin. He couldn't contain the smile that spread across his face.

'It certainly is.'

'I thought we'd looked everywhere, where did you find it?' He turned the package around in his hands.

'It was all down to Peggy.' Karina told him, not taking the credit herself.

'And who is Peggy? She one of your lot?' asked Marlowe.

'Sort of, Peggy's a member of the Drug Squad. She's a sniffer dog.'

'Ha, bloody ha, thanks for stringing that one out.'

'You wouldn't have found it. It was well hidden in the under floor insulation of the mobile home, tucked well into the fibreglass matting.'

'How much do you reckon its worth?' Marlowe asked, as he weighed the parcel up and down in his hands like a pair of scales.

'The wholesale value is around £40K per kilo, so I'd guess that would make it in the region of £80K, give or take.'

'Bloody hell,' he passed the package back, 'best keep it safe then.'

'It'd be worth double that on the streets when it had been diluted.'

'Diluted? What with, baking powder?'

'Sometimes, these days they use so-called specialist cutting agents like cockroach pesticide, dog worming powder and phenacetin.'

'Phenawotsit? Never heard of it.'

'Well Phenacetin, now that *is* evil. Believe it or not it was the world's first synthetic painkiller. The stuff was banned in the 1980s because of its horrific side effects and on top of that it was linked with cancer.'

'Nasty stuff. Did you manage to get any prints off the package?'

'Plenty, the trouble is they're not in our system, but that's to be expected when you think it's come from half way around the world.'

'Not what I wanted to hear.' Marlowe stood and walked across to the open window hoping to catch a draught.

'I hadn't finished,' continued Karina and Marlowe turned. 'There was a clear left hand index finger and thumb print…ready for this? They belong to Patrick Murphy.' Karina smiled.

'Yes - we've got the bugger, Karina you've made an old man happy.'

'Are you going to bring him in?'

'Eventually, but we'll leave him be for now, he's not going anywhere. I want to tie him into the Finch and Logan situation. When we get the sod sent down I want to make sure he stays there. In the meantime I'm going to have a cup of tea to celebrate.'

Chapter 18

'What do you reckon, Tanya, you think it's worth giving it a go?' asked DC Kristianson.

'Who did you say reported him missing again?'

Lee knew by heart, but checked his notes all the same. 'His wife, Patricia O'Hara according to the MISPER had just found out she was pregnant. She thought maybe that's why he'd done a runner.'

'Well, it's the best lead we've got, what have we got to lose? Let's go and see if she's still around.'

Lee was all smiles as Tanya grabbed her coat and bag and led the way out of the office. 'Yes, a result,' he said under his breath.

Mrs O'Hara's home was a two storey, three bed roomed terrace house down Perth Street, just off the busy thoroughfare off Chanterlands Avenue. Lee pulled the pool car into the kerb side directly opposite Mrs O'Hara's home. Not a million miles away from where Tanya lived.

'How old do you reckon she'll be now?' Lee asked as he stared out of the car window.

'You do the sums. If she was twenty in 1978 - that'd make her about fifty five now.'

They left the vehicle, crossed the road and Tanya knocked on the glass panel door. The silhouette of a woman approached the door. She opened it slightly on the safety chain and spoke. 'I don't need any double glazing and I already have a conservatory...'

'Mrs O'Hara?' Tanya interrupted.

'Who wants to know? ' She asked warily.

'My name is DC Etherington and this is my colleague DC Kristianson.' Both officers held their warrant cards to the narrow gap between the door and frame. 'May we have a word, please?'

The door was closed shut, Lee looked towards Tanya, then they heard a metallic clinking as the safety chain was removed and the door fully opened. A slim, middle aged woman with short cropped hair, wearing far too much makeup stood before them. She smiled, stood to one side and allowed them to pass, gesturing for them to go through to the kitchen-diner. 'Please,' she said pointing to the chairs around the dining table. 'What's this about?'

'Mrs O'Hara, what I'm about to ask you may seem strange...even come as a bit of a shock.'

'Not much can shock me, love, I've seen and heard it all.'

'Am I correct in thinking you are the same Mrs O'Hara who in 1978 filed a missing person report on your husband Kevin?' She nodded.

'Well bugger me; don't tell me he's turned up after all these years?' The expression on her face was one of neither joy nor surprise. Her expression remained impassive as she walked across to the dresser, and picked up a packet of cigarettes. 'You don't mind do you? She didn't wait for a response, took out a cigarette, picked up a cheap plastic lighter and lit up. Blue smoke from her mouth curled up to the ceiling as she spoke. 'I haven't given the bugger any thought in years. At first I thought he'd just gone on a bender, or cleared off because I was pregnant, but then...I didn't know what to think. When Sean was born things were hard at first but eventually we just got on with our lives.'

'The thing is, Mrs O'Hara what we have to tell you may not be the news you are expecting,' said Lee, 'but it may give you an answer after all these years.' Mrs O'Hara suddenly paled.

'The bugger's dead, isn't he?' she said as she sat down in a vacant chair.

'The council have been doing some excavation work, and the remains of a man who broadly fits the description you gave of your husband back in 1978, has been discovered. Unfortunately due to the length of time the remains lay undiscovered visual identification isn't possible.'

'How do you know it's him then?' she looked puzzled.

'That's the problem; we don't…not for sure. What we need to be certain is a DNA sample, do you still have any of your husband's belongings?' asked Tanya.

'Sorry love, I got rid of it all years back, didn't see any point in hanging on to it.'

'What about your son, do you think he would be willing to give us a DNA sample?' asked Tanya.

'Maybe, I don't see why not, no harm in asking I suppose. Fancy a cup of coffee?' Mrs O'Hara asked.

Tanya and Lee gratefully accepted the coffee out of politeness, although Mrs O'Hara appeared to be in control of things, they had their doubts, after all they had let the *skeleton out of the closet*. 'Thanks again for the coffee, and if you can ask your son to come into the station when he gets a free moment it would be appreciated.' Tanya gave Mrs O'Hara one of her business cards, thanked her again and they left the woman to her rekindled thoughts.

Chapter 19

It was a glorious day for being at the seaside, if you were a holidaymaker. A warm sunny day with hardly a breeze, even the North Sea looked blue instead of its usual grey colour. 'We used to come here a lot when I was a kid,' the fat bouncer said as he and Keane drove along the seafront promenade at Hornsea, his feet resting high on the dashboard.

'Never been one for seaside myself, too much bleedin' sand. And get your feet off my dash.' The bouncer looked in surprise, Keane was deadly serious, the bouncer tutted and did as he was told. Keane parked the Range Rover short of the caravan site and they approached on foot, so as not to arouse suspicion from nosey neighbours. 'Well it looks as if we've had a wasted trip.' They had a clear view of the mobile home. The entire structure looked as if it was wrapped in plastic blue and white crime scene tape, there was no point in going any further.

'Looks like its wrapped for Christmas, just missing the fairy lights,' the fat bouncer said. 'What do you reckon?'

'I reckon we had a wasted bleedin' trip. If there was owt hidden in there the cops will have it. Shit. Let's piss off back.'

'Your uncle isn't going to be very happy,' the bouncer said, shaking his head.

'Tell me about it, I wouldn't fancy being in what's left of Anderson's shoes.'

'So you reckon your uncle will top him? Fatty asked.

'I don't really need to answer that do I?' Keane returned to the Range Rover as his mobile phone started singing out the theme tune to the *A-Team*.

'Speak of the devil,' he said to his oppo as he checked the display before answering. 'Uncle Pat...no there was fuck all there, looks like the coppers beat us to it...yeah, we're on the way back, see you later.' Keane let Fatty do the driving, while he sat looking out of the side window as the bouncer concentrated on the winding road. 'Not a happy chappie,' he turned to the bouncer, 'wants us round at the house.' Keane turned to look out of the window once more.

The evening was drawing in as they duly arrived at Murphy's country home. Keane left the bouncer in the kitchen with a mug of coffee, while he went through to the lounge, he wasn't very long. Just long enough to receive his instructions from his uncle. Keane looked sullen as he came back into the kitchen. He poured himself a coffee and sat down at the table.

'Well, what now?' asked Fatty.

Keane passed across a bundle of keys. 'Take Uncle Pat's car down to the stable, see you in a minute.' Fatty didn't argue, he just did as he was told, he drove the 4x4 down the gravel path and parked up outside the stable.

To his surprise the stable door was not locked. Nothing could have prepared him for the sight and smell that greeted him as he opened the wooden door and went inside. Anderson's broken and beaten corpse hung from the wooden beam, the draft from the open door made the figure sway from side to side, as if was hung on the gallows. Fatty stood staring at the swaying body. Quietly, Keane opened the door, edged forward without making a sound and stood directly behind him and gently touched the back of Fatty's neck.

The bouncer nearly jumped out of his skin with fright. 'Jesus, Sean, you bastard,' he said as he turned sharply with his heart beating thirteen to a dozen.

'Wuss. Cop a hold of these and put 'em on.' Keane threw across a pair of ex-army overalls.

'What the fuck do I need to wear these for?'

'Just put them on.'

'Bit bleedin' tight.' Hopping about from one foot to the other, the fat bouncer struggled as he tried to fit a too large body into a too small suit.

'Stop moaning, just get the things on and then roll that sheet out.'

'Do we really need to wear em?' He was making a meal of getting suited.

'You'll be glad you are when you see what Uncle Patrick wants us to do. Just going to the motor.' The bouncer wasn't the squeamish type but hoped he wouldn't be long; he didn't want to be left on his own with a hanging corpse.

Fatty heard the Range Rover door open and close again. Keane came back inside carrying a large heavy canvas hold-haul. He set the bag on the floor and locked the stable door behind him. The bouncer watched with interest, the bag was unzipped and Keane took out what was inside.

'Oh no, you must be fucking joking! I'm not having any of that! For fucks sake *Chainsaw Massacre* aint for me, I'm off.' He started to unfasten the suit; this was not what he'd signed up for.

'No you fucking don't, you're already in this up to your bloody neck, and what does it matter he's FUCKING DEAD! Not going to be bothered is he!' If Keane was honest about it, he wasn't really relishing the task himself. He'd already had a similar conversation with his Uncle and was told he'd do "as he was feckin told".

'Well I'm not using the fucking saw.'

'For such a tough looking bloke you can be a right tart at times. Just get the fucker down while I see how this thing works.'

The bouncer looked at the limp figure dangling like a marionette at the end of the rope and shook his head. 'It was your own bleedin' fault,' he said to the corpse as if expecting an answer. He adjusted the plastic sheet until it was centrally placed underneath the swaying figure. He walked to where the end of the rope was tied fast, unwound it from the cleat and took the weight. The pulley fixed to the roof rafter squeaked as it was placed under the duress of the full weight of the body. 'Shit,' the bouncer called out as he lost his footing on the shiny plastic sheet and let go of the rope and the body dropped to the floor in a broken heap.

'Haven't hurt him have you?' The ice was broken and there was laughter all round.

Brumm, splut, splut, brummmmmm. 'Think I've got the hang of this now,' said Keane waving the heavy mechanical saw around like a light sabre from *Star Wars*. He cut the choke and the saw fell quiet, he put it down and went over to the bag again. 'I think we deserve a couple of these before we get started. What do you say?' He passed across a bottle of Famous Grouse Scotch Whisky.

'What does your Uncle want us to do with Anderson when we've finished? He took a deep swig of the whisky.

'Didn't I tell you he's just opened a butchers shop…'

The bouncer spit the whisky out all over the corpse. 'Oh tell me you *are* taking the piss?' Keane just couldn't keep a straight face and burst out laughing. 'Sean you are such a fucking wanker, you had me going then,' he joined in the laughter. 'Mind you I wouldn't put it past him if he thought he'd get away with it, just like that *Sweeney Todd* bloke in *Oliver*.'

Keane didn't know if the bouncer was serious in his reference to *Sweeney Todd* or just being plain daft but didn't correct him. 'You're not wrong there, if there was a quid to be made…give us a swig of the Scotch.'

By the time the whisky bottle had been passed back and forth between them several times the inhibitions of both men faded away.

'You ready?' He pulled the starter cord, brummmm, brummmm, the chainsaw sang out, brummmm.

'Ready as I'll ever be.' Fatty grimaced at the thought of what was about to happen.

'Ok, here we go, think I'll start with an easy bit, hold his arm up.' The bouncer grabbed the cold waxy hand and held it high of the floor. Brummmmm.

''Fucks sake, I don't think I can do this,' the bouncer said as Anderson's right arm came away in his hands, he retched, the whisky came back up and he swallowed.

116

'Just grit your teeth and get on with, or I'll beat you up with the soggy end.'

And so the black humour continued. Left arm, legs jointed at the ankles and knees until all that was left was a torso with a head still attached, but not for long. Brummmm, it rolled and stopped at the Fatty's feet, dead orbs staring up, or would have if there had been any eyes there to stare up. This time the whisky didn't stay down.

'What about his bonce, won't someone recognise him?' Fatty said when he'd regained his composure.

'Jesus, have you seen the state of it? No fucker will recognise that mess.'

'I still don't get why your uncle had to do that to him.' He stood staring down at the dead sorry face.

'You heard that story about the three monkeys? *Hear no evil*, that was Finch with his ears lobbed off, *speak no evil,* that was Logan with his laughing gear sorted and Anderson, well he was all three, *hear no evil, speak no evil and see…* ears, mouth and eyes.'

'Fucking evil.' He shook his head. It had become a habit during the night's work.

'Who you on about?' Keane said as he grabbed a bundle of hair, picked the head up and dropped it in a bin bag.

'You're fucking uncle that's who.'

'Yeah well I'll leave it up to you tell him. Let's get these joints wrapped up,' he threw the wrapped-up head to Fatty like a rugby ball.'

Chapter 20

Mornings in the club were for the cleaners, but in the late afternoons things at the *Snake Pit* changed. This was when things started to come to life. The place began to buzz in anticipation of the night to come as the staff drifted in to prepare for the evening.

'Be careful!' Murphy yelled at a young waitress, as she struggled rattling her way towards the bar with an overloaded tray of glasses. 'If you break any it'll come out of your bloody wages.' The girl looked as if she wished she could crawl away and die. Keane, never one to miss an opportunity with the opposite sex went over to help.

'Give it here,' he said reaching out. 'What's your name?' Keane asked as he took the heavy tray off the girl and placed it on the bar top.

'Emma,' she replied nervously, the conversation didn't go any further.'

'Sean, office if you can *spare* the time.' Keane smiled at the girl, picked up two whisky glasses from the bar and followed his uncle into the office. The girl would keep until his uncle wasn't around. 'Close the feckin door behind you,' snapped Murphy, 'how many times have I told you not to feck with the staff?' Keane shrugged, he was used to being rebuffed by his uncle. He placed the whisky glasses on the desk, took out his cigarettes and lit up a Marlborough red top. Dropping into a chair, he waited for the one-sided conversation to continue. 'Did you get shut?' he asked referring to Anderson's body parts.

'He's spread all over East Yorkshire, Uncle Pat,' he sat back in the chair, blowing smoke rings that circled upwards to the low ceiling.

'We'll have no come back then?' He opened a desk drawer, took out a bottle of Famous Grouse Whisky, two glasses and poured large measures.

'No problem, Uncle Pat. Me and Fatty spread him from here to Aldborough on the coast.' Keane reached over and picked up his whisky, sat back with his legs out in front crossed at the ankles, sipped and continued to blow blue smoke to the ceiling. 'I reckon some bits will turn up, but nothing to connect him to us.'

'The Manchester lot, they've been chasing me for payment again, it's due in 48hours.' Murphy took out one of his miniature cigars and lit up adding to the room's pollution problem.

'We got the cash to cover it?' asked Keane as he held the glass high, studying the amber liquid.

'Aye lad we've got money enough. But I don't like to splash out with the best part of 100k for feck all. So I want to know if the coppers have the stuff, if so where, and I want it back.'

'Christ, Uncle Pat, we can't just walk into the cop shop and say, "excuse me, please can we have our drugs back!"'

'You don't take the piss out of me, son,' he growled. 'Where there's a will there's a way…I know I can rely on you.'

The problem was now Keane's and he wasn't happy about it. How the hell was he going to retrieve the merchandise from a police station?

Chapter 21

'Who do you fancy winning the rugby at the weekend, FC or Rovers?' Police Constable Nigel Nunn asked his colleague Graham 'Nocker Norton, referring to the local derby between Hull's two rugby league clubs, Hull FC and Hull Kingston Rovers. They stood by the squad car having a crafty fag.

'To be honest I don't give a ...' He never finished the reply. A smartly dressed posh looking woman approached, with a dog on a lead in one hand, and carrying a black plastic bin liner in the other.

'Excuse me, officers,' said Mrs Posh. Nunn turned his face away, blowing smoke into the wind.

'Yes, love, what can we do for you?' Nocker asked as he skilfully cupped his cigarette end in the palm of his hand, craftily dropping the butt to the floor and grinding it out with his boot.

'My, Billy here,' she pointed to the waggy tailed mutt, 'just went down the river bank and came back dragging this.' She passed across the plastic bag.

'And what have we got here,' asked Nocker as he took hold of the bin bag. He opened it wide, Nunn edged forward and looked over his shoulder into the open bag. 'Sh...,' Nunn stifled the word, but he needn't have bothered.

'No need to be embarrassed, that's the exact same word I used myself, dear,' said Mrs Posh.

'Is that what I think it is?' Nunn pulled a face as he spoke.

'Depends on what you think it is. I'll tell you what I think it is; it's a chunk of forearm. See that there?' he pointed to the wrist joint of his own hand, 'looks like that nobbly bone to me'.

'Can you show us where you actually found it please, love?' Nocker asked.

Mrs Posh and Billy led the way along the grass riverbank of the River Hull. 'My Billy went down about here.' It was low tide and the brown slimy mud came halfway up the grassy bank.

'Well it doesn't look like there's anything else down there.' Neither officer had any intention of venturing down the slippery slope into the mud. 'If we can have your details, love, just in case we need to contact you.'

'Will it be in the paper?' asked Mrs Posh.

'I wouldn't be surprised,' Nocker replied, screwing the neck of the bin bag tight. Holding the bag at arm's length he carried it to the car, popped the boot and stored the macabre find.

***

'Bet you can't guess what we've got in here, sarge?' PC Norton said as he unceremoniously dumped the bin bag on the custody desk.

'Well, judging from the smell it's not my clean washing,' he replied as he wrinkled his nose and reached for the bag. 'For fuck's sake,' he said as he looked inside, 'good job I've already eaten, where did you find it?' Nocker and Nunn re-told the circumstances of how they came into possession of a lump of human flesh. The conversation was interrupted when the desk phone rang. It was the communications room. 'Cleeves,' he said into the receiver, he listened, quiet. 'Hell fire what going on…ok, tell them to bring it in and I'll get the duty quack down here. Well, lads,' he said to Nocker and Nunn, 'seems we've got another bit to go with yours.'

'What shall we do with it, sarge?' asked Nocker.

'Sign it in and stick it in the fridge 'till the doctor gets here.'

'You want me to do CPR? 'cos I think we're a bit late and the doc won't do much good.'

'Don't be lairy, remember to empty the fridge before you put it in. Mind you, if you see anything with DCI's name on it you can leave it where it is.'

Chapter 22

Tanya was sat at her over loaded desk, sorting through the documents relating to a spate of stolen credit cards that DS Bright had dumped on her desk when the phone rang. 'DC Etherington,' she said into the handset as she sorted documents one-handed.

'Tanya, it's Trevor on the desk, looks like your lucks changed, there's some young bloke in reception asking for you.'

'Do you know who it is, did they give a name?'

'Oh I know who it is alright.' She could "hear" the smile on his face at the other end of the phone.

'Sergeant, will you please tell *me* who it is then.' Getting annoyed.

'Well, are you ready for this? his name's Sean Keane.' Silence. 'You get that?'

'What on earth does he want with me?'

'If you get yourself through here you can find out can't you.' She heard the phone click back on the cradle.

Tanya was intrigued. Sean Keene, the nephew of one of Hull's most notorious villains wanting to see her, she wondered what the hell it was about and stood up from the desk. She smoothed down her trousers, tucked her hair behind her ears and checked her appearance in the computer monitor. Armed with her A4 notepad, she went to satisfy her curiosity. Of course Tanya knew of Keane, every police officer in the city knew of him and of his reputation, but she'd never met him. The DC was quite taken aback by what she saw, a thirty something man in a designer suit who stood leaning against the reception desk. From the back view Tanya was impressed, tall with a slim build and carried the suit well. He seemed to sense her approach and turned. She changed her mind when Keane smiled with his ferret like face. She wondered how such an individual could be such a cold callous bastard.

'Mr Keane, I'm DC Tanya Etherington, I believe you want to see me?' She smiled and held out her hand.

'It's the other way round love.' Keane seemed to be quite amused as he reached out to shake hands. Tanya was puzzled. 'You've been to see to my, Ma', she reckons you've found my old man, or what's left of him.'

'Ah, now I get it, sorry the penny didn't drop. I didn't associate your name with your mother's being different.

'Seeing as though the old man was supposed to have buggered off and left us, I changed it to my Grandmother's maiden name. Anyway, can we get this DNA over and done with, I've a business to get on with.' *I bet you have* thought Tanya, *crippling people and slicing their ears off.*

'Would you come this way, please?' Tanya stepped back. Keane smiled as he followed her through the security door further into the station, it made a change for him being there helping with their enquiries voluntarily. Tanya inclined her head towards the visitor's suite and gestured towards the seats. 'Would you like a coffee or anything?'

'No thanks, let's just get on with it.' He stood in the centre of the room ignoring the offer to sit.

'Before I go and get the DNA kit, Mr Keane, do we by any chance have your DNA on record already?'

'I shouldn't think so, love, I've never been arrested.' *Yet* she thought. Tanya left Keane alone in the room feeling somewhat jubilant; Sean Keene's DNA on record and given voluntarily this was definitely a coup. Tanya returned a couple of minutes later with the DNA kit.

'This won't take long.' With a long plastic stick with a cotton bud end, she swabbed the inside of Keane's mouth and secured the swab in sterile plastic test-tube. 'All done.'

'That it?' asked Keane.

'Yes, that's it. Thanks very much, Mr Keane, I appreciate you coming in. As soon as we have the results I'll let you and your mother know.' Tanya showed Keane to the front lobby, he gave Sergeant Cleeves a nod of the head. Tanya shook hands with Keane and watched him leave. Then wiped the palm of her hand down her trousers.

'Well what do you reckon?' Cleeves asked the detective.

'Smarmy sod if you ask me, sarge, wouldn't trust him as far as I could throw him.'

***

In the back room of The Carlton, a private members club, two men sat huddled across a battle scarred table, trying to avoid putting their elbows in the puddles of booze. 'Piss off, not a fucking chance.' The voices were low, Sean Keane's was one of the voices.

'All I'm asking is that you make a little something disappear, not too much to ask is it?'

'If I get found out they'll not only give me the bullet, I'll go down the fucking road as well,' he shook his head from side to side, 'no fucking way.'

'You owe me. Do this one thing and not only will nobody know your lad's a junky but you'll have a few quid in your skyrocket as well,' said Murphy's nephew as he leaned in closer.

'You make it sound the easiest thing in the world. Your round I think.'

'Fuck,' said Keane and went to the bar for the third time. Every time was his round. Keane returned with drinks. 'Here you go, mate,' he said with exaggerated friendliness, not really meaning it as he placed them on the table adding to the spillage already there.

'I'm not saying it can't be done or hasn't already been done, it's just that I've never done it.'

'Does that mean you're going to do it? You fucking star!' Keane sat back in his chair.

'It'll cost, I'm not doing it for fuck all.'

'Two grand, how does that sound?' Keane was confident the deal would be accepted.

'On your bike, make it five and I'm in. It'll top up my pension fund.' Keane reached across the table and shook the man's hand to seal the deal. 'Your round I think.'

'My pleasure.' For once Keane wasn't bothered about always being the one in the chair. Ten minutes later he left, leaving Sergeant Trevor Cleeves alone nursing his pint.

Chapter 23

'Morning, Magnum,' Sergeant Cleeves jibed as the DCI entered the station through the rear door.

'Good morning to you, Trevor. Anything interesting come in overnight?' he asked as he walked across to the custody officer's desk and slapped down his briefcase, making the Sergeant's coffee splash over the rim of his mug.'

'Steady up, Chief Inspector,' Cleeves grabbed some paper towels from under the desk and started to mop up while Marlowe looked on smiling. 'You won't have that smile on your face for long when I tell you what's going on.' Marlowe sighed and waited, it was bound to be a long story. 'Late yesterday afternoon after you'd swanned off, Nocker and Nunn brought a lump of meat in, well it was actually a piece of forearm.'

'How did you know it was a forearm?' Marlowe asked.

'It was still wearing a watch!' Marlowe knew he should have known better than to ask, Cleeves as usual went into a fit of hysterical laughter at his own joke.

'An arm?' Marlowe asked when the laughter had subsided.

'As I said, Nunn and Nocker were presented with an arm in a bin bag by an old lady. Her dog found it on the bank of the River Hull, near the bridge on Clough Road.' Cleeves struggled to recover his composure. 'Less than an hour later another bin bag turned up in the dyke on Orchard Park, one of our lads found it.'

'I'm waiting for the joke,' said Marlowe into the silence that followed Cleeves' statement.

'No joke, Phil, this time it was a bloody left foot, roughly cut off at the ankle.'

'Where are the parts now?'

'Down at the mortuary…waiting for the rest of their owner to claim them.'

'I don't know what this city is turning into, Trev. Getting more like London every day. I'll get someone to ring the pathologist to see what's going on. Keep me posted if any more turn up.' Dismemberment was an unusual occurrence in Hull, not unheard of but nevertheless not your every day crime. Marlowe kept his fingers crossed, hoping that it was just a prank by medical students or some other idiots with access to fresh body parts.

The DCI entered the squad room with a flourish, if a cropped haired middle-aged man can do such a thing. 'Mornin'' one and all,' he said only to be met with a few mumbles and groans

'Morning, boss,' Tanya said as she looked up from the computer monitor.

'Glad to see good manners still exist, I was beginning to have doubts about the younger generation. Tanya, Lee, give me a couple of minutes and come through.' Lee looked up from the computer screen and caught the DCI's eye. 'Coffee would be nice, strong no sugar and not from the vending machine,' Marlowe smiled to himself and disappeared before the young detective had a chance to make up some excuse or other.

'He always does that, never asks you...always me,' Lee grumbled looking over the other side of the desk to Tanya.

'Well if you're getting the boss one, I'll have mine black... please.' Lee tut tutted and went to the canteen in search of fresh coffee.

'Well don't stand there on ceremony, take a seat.' Marlowe said when Lee returned with a tray of coffee mugs. Tanya had learned the hard way, and took the tubular plastic chair while Lee sank low and undignified into the sofa. 'They tell me you had a visitor yesterday?' Marlowe sat back in his chair holding his coffee between both hands.

'It was an experience, I know that much. When Mrs O'Hara said she'd ask her son to come in for the DNA test, I definitely wasn't expecting Sean Keane to turn up.'

'It's got to be a first for that family, someone actually coming into the station without wearing a pair of handcuffs. 'Is this from the canteen?' Marlowe asked before sipping the hot drink. No response from the young DC who couldn't see the DCI was trying to wind him up. 'What did you make of him?'

'I was surprised, for a sadistic thug I thought he came over quite well, considering,' replied Tanya.

'And you, Lee, are you any further on in establishing if anyone knew about the bungled bank job?'

Lee was feeling put out, not only for being sent on the coffee run like an errand boy but also because he was the one who established the link between Mrs O'Hara and the bag of bones spread out in the morgue. 'Not really, boss, it was so long ago anyone who might have seen or heard anything are long gone from the area.' Marlowe nodded in agreement.

Before the meeting progressed further a knock on the door interrupted the proceedings. DI Gowan stuck his head around the door frame. 'It's alright, Dave, come in we've just about finished here.'

'Thought I'd get in first and spare you Cleeves' jokes and let you know more body parts have been found.'

'I'm waiting for the punch-line,' said the DCI.

'No punch-line, we haven't got the hands yet! Sorry couldn't resist. Seriously all told, so far we've got a lump of thigh, shoulder to elbow and a left foot, if we had a hand at least we might have been able to get some prints...' Gowan's mobile vibrated in his pocket, he took it out and glanced at the screen, 'just got to take this,' he muttered and walked out of the office into the corridor. Thirty seconds later he was back. 'I stand corrected, we now have a right hand in good condition, I'll get it finger printed as soon as the Doc's had a look at it.'

'So it's not looking like some sort of prank, shit.' Marlowe said sullenly.

'Not looking that way, uniform made enquiries at Hull Royal Infirmary and the Castle Hill Hospitals, everything checked out. All the spare bits that have to be incinerated are logged, nothing missing.'

'What about undertakers?' Tanya asked.

'Same there, Tanya, nothing missing, all bodies complete and waiting for dispatch. The pathologist says all the parts we have are the same blood group, the lab is running DNA as a formality but expect them all to come back with the same profile.'

'How were the limbs removed, surgically?' asked Lee.

'Hardly a neat job, seems they were all hacked off.' Gowan smiled, all part of the job.

'As if we haven't got enough nutters out there. I'll leave this with you then, Dave.'

'No problem, boss, I'll get Jenny on it. It'll give her a chance to get away from the credit card business for a while.' *That's about right* thought Tanya, who had been doing most of the leg work relating to the credit card fiasco. Lee, Tanya and DI Gowan left the DCI to his paperwork. 'Hang on you two don't go rushing off,' Dave said before they had a chance to disappear. 'Tanya, you ok with skelly and the Keane thing?'

'No problems at the minute, sir,' she replied confidently.

'In that case you won't need Lee.'

'Yes…but…' her confidence wavered.

'Don't worry, if you need anything give me a shout, don't forget Jonno has been around the block a few times, he's a mine of useless information.'

'I heard that, SIR,' Jonno piped up from around the side of the vending machine, with a big emphasis on the sir.

'I was just telling, Tanya, if she needs anything she can always count on your vast knowledge and experience.'

'Yeah, ok, inspector," laughed Jonno, "I get your drift.'

'See if DS Bright is in the station and tell her I want a word,' Gowan told Lee and then he went off to have a word with Sergeant Cleeves.

***

The sun was shining through the conservatory windows. Keane tilted the Venetian blind. 'Don't suppose you've seen Ma lately have you?' he asked his uncle.

'Not for a while, lad, suppose I should give her a call sometime, why do you ask?'

'She had the coppers around the other day, it seems they might have found my old man.'

The comment threw Murphy off kilter, this he was not expecting. Ever. June 14th 1978 was the last time Patrick Murphy had seen his brother in-law. It was the day his sister, full of excitement had broken the news to the family of her pregnancy. It was jubilation all round, except for Murphy who had always thought her husband was a loser.

For the sake of his sister, Murphy had welcomed O'Hara into the family, and in a minor way into the family business. Initially he had his uses, a good man with locks, any locks, there weren't many that he couldn't persuade to give up their secrets. For a time things seemed to be running along without any major problems, then much to Murphy's disappointment the engagement was announced. Once married to Murphy's sister, Jean, and O'Hara his feet were well and truly under the table. Then gradually things started to change, he began to get above himself, wanting a more active role in the family business. It was not going to happen.

The opportunity to rid the family of the waster came about by chance. A complicated scheme to break into the Midland Bank was developed. This was to be a two man job, although Murphy disliked O'Hara, he wanted to keep the job low profile and accepted he had to use his brother in-law. A tunnel was to be excavated between the disused subterranean ladies toilet on the corner the Boulevard and Hessle Road junction and into the basement of the bank, approximately six metres away. Using a van bought legitimately out of the Hull Daily Mail classified ads, it was duly decaled up in livery as belonging to Yorkshire Water, and with Murphy and O'Hara dressed in the appropriate overalls work began. The work was carried out during daylight hours, no one was going to query what was going on, after all what was unusual with what they were doing. It wasn't as if they were going to break into a bank. Murphy planned on digging the one metre square tunnel at a length of two metres a day, with the final push at night, again it wouldn't look out of place for contractors to be working during the evening.

Days one and two went as planned, things were still going ok with Murphy and his brother in-law taking alternative shifts in the tunnel with a pick, shovel and pneumatic drill...then three metres in, the roof of the tunnel collapsed while O'Hara was laid on his stomach trying to use the pneumatic drill. He'd managed to miss serious injury by swiftly crawling backwards out of the subterranean dungeon filling with debris and dust, Murphy had grabbed him by the ankles aiding his escape. Then in a calculated moment Murphy saw his chance to rid the family of the waster once and for all. O'Hara lay on his front coughing and spluttering, Murphy had picked up a brick and with one swift movement brought it down hard on the back of his brother in-law's head. O'Hara was then unceremoniously shoved back into the tunnel, and Murphy had attacked the bricks above with a sledge hammer, covering the body in rubble.

'You alright, Uncle Pat? Keane asked Murphy who sat seemingly in a daze.

Murphy came back to the here and now. 'Aye lad, just thinking about things...it was a long time ago.'

'Tell me about it, you could have knocked me down with a feather when Ma told me, then when she sprung it on me the coppers wanted me to do a DNA test to make a comparison well...'

'I hope you told her to feck off?' Murphy was not back in control.

'No, I went in to the nick yesterday and did a test; I need to know one way or another.'

'You did feckin what? You stupid feckin little bastard.'
Keane was used to his Uncle's outbursts, but this was something
different. 'Have you got no feckin brains inside that head off yours?'
He walked across with still aching ribs and poured himself a whisky.

'I was only…' Keane stammered out.

'I don't care what you was only trying to do, you've just
given the law your feckin DNA!' Murphy stood and sipped the fiery
amber liquid. 'You'd better watch yerself, lad, if they tie your
bleedin' DNA profile to Logan or Finch you're in shit creek.' With a
sigh he dropped into his chair. Keane, lost for words also attacked
the whisky bottle. All he wanted to do was keep his Ma happy, he
hadn't thought about the consequences.

Chapter 24

Lee sat staring at his computer screen. 'Sarge, I've just had an email from the forensic people, it turns out the dismembered body parts belong to someone called Ian Anderson. They also found some hairs in one of the packets, not human or dog hair but they're testing to see what they might belong to.'

'Let's have a look,' Lee passed across the file it didn't take long to scan through the details, 'you'd better show this to the DI, while I check if any more joints of meat have turned up.' To her dismay the overnighters showed most of the bits had indeed turned up, the jigsaw was almost complete…all but the torso and head.

The discovery of the latest grisly finds prompted Marlowe to call an immediate briefing with his senior officers. They gathered around Jonno's desk, although Jonno was only a DC, Marlowe had known him a long time and rated him highly as a police officer and was often included in such meetings. Before and after pictures of Logan, Finch and Anderson were fixed to the white board facing into the room. It looked like an advertisement for the local butchers, the board plastered with 8inch by 10inch colour photographs of dismembered limbs and disfigurement. Marlowe sat on the corner of Jonno's desk facing the team. 'Finch, Logan and Anderson, one common denominator, and as we all know things have moved on a stage further. Who's going first?' asked the DCI.

'Got to be Murphy?' said Jenny as she walked across the room and opened the window wide.

'That'll do for starters…' Marlowe waited for her to carry on.

'If you think about it logically, who else could be responsible?' she said as she returned to her chair.

'I agree,' said Marlowe loosening his tie, the opened window wasn't doing much good, 'but as we are we don't have anything concrete.'

Jenny leaned forward resting on her elbows. 'We've got the statement Finch gave the DI and Jonno.'

'No good, Jenny, the bloke was frightened for his mate, wouldn't sign anything official. Just wanted to give us the heads up.'

Dave Gowan put a damper on things. 'Is it getting warmer in here or is it just me?' No one answered.

'However we do have the drugs with Murphy's dabs on them.' said Marlowe.

'Bring him in?' suggested Jonno.

'I wasn't planning to yet, but now it's turned into a murder investigation we'll have to or the Super will have me cleaning the toilets. But first I want the *Snake Pit* searched, top to bottom, see if we can find any trace of Finch or Logan. Dave, get a warrant sorted will you, before you bring him in.'

'Just for the club?'

'For now, I don't think with what we've got so far we'd get a warrant for his home 'till we bring him in and besides we don't want that twat of a solicitor on our backs.'

'I'll get Tanya to check with the pathologist and see if he knows what was used to dismember the body,' said Dave Gowan.

'And I want the CSEs lot around Anderson's place ASAP,' said Marlowe. 'As things stand we've got more than enough to go on, but no real evidence so let's get cracking.' The DCI stood, a sign the briefing was being brought to a close.

Marlowe returned to his own office, and by some strange occurrence wasn't interrupted any further, giving him the opportunity to partially clear his desk of the daily influx of paperwork overflowing from the in-tray. He sat back in his chair and stretched his arms above his head. There was a quick knock on the door and Gowan stuck his head around the corner of the door frame.

'Coming for a pint, Phil?' asked the DI, who only ever used Marlowe's Christian name in private.

'Not tonight thanks, Dave, I'm knackered.' Marlowe reached for his back pocket and took out his wallet and took out a ten pound note. 'Get a round in on me.' Gowan looked at the note and them back to Marlowe. 'I get the message,' he said and passed across another ten pounds.

'Cheers, Phil, have a good night.' And then he was gone with the DCIs money. Home was the next move Marlowe was going to make.

***

'Why do you always ask me to come for a drink when the DI's going to do karaoke?' Tanya asked Lee as they pushed shoulder to shoulder to reach the table where Dave Gowan was holding court.

'Thursday's always karaoke night,' Lee replied.

'Got you a drink already, courtesy of the boss,' Gowan said as they sat down.

'Cheers, sir,' Tanya picked up her wine and soda.

'You *can* call me Dave, we are off duty.' She smiled, wishing she were somewhere else as Dave Gowan looked at the karaoke play list, deciding which Roy Orbison song he was going to start with. Tanya checked their position in relation to the stage. In her short time with the squad, experience had taught her not to sit too close to the sound system when the DI was singing. Not wanting to seem a kill joy she stayed for another drink and suffered the DI's rendition of *Pretty Woman* then discretely slipped away.

Tanya parked the car on the wide grass verge outside of her flat and climbed the stairs to the top floor. She was looking forward to having a relaxing bath, a bite to eat and sitting in front of the television chilling out until bedtime, which wasn't too far in the future. She still felt the need to keep making a good impression with her peers as well as the boss, things had been going well since she transferred to the big city and she wanted it to stay that way.

Chapter 25

Sean Keane, registered as the official key holder of the *Snake Pit*, was surprised and pissed off when the club cleaning supervisor disturbed his sleep by ringing his mobile. He reached out, fumbling and found his mobile, the time showed it was only 8.30am. 'Yeah, what,' he mumbled sleepily into the mobile.

'Mr Keane, it's Brendan at the club,' the supervisor said warily.

'This better be good...what time is it?' Keane sat up, scratching his head.

'Half past eight, Mr Keane, the police are here I don't know what to do.'

'Say again,' said Keane, sleepily hoping he'd misheard.

'The police, they've got a warrant to search the club, they're all over the place.' Keane gave no thanks, just hung up and pressed the speed dial key to his uncle.

Murphy didn't have time to wait for a taxi and despite having one arm in fibreglass cast, took to the wheel of his Mercedes and reached the club minutes before his nephew. He fumed to himself when he saw the police vehicles in his car park. Murphy parked up between a battered Scene of Crimes Unit vehicle and a police squad car which he gave a bloody great kick, denting the door.

'Who the feck let this lot in?' Murphy shouted to no one in particular as he stormed through the front doors barging a uniformed officer out of the way.

'Sorry, Mr Murphy,' replied the cleaning supervisor as he rushed to greet him. 'They were waiting outside when I got here to open up. I couldn't stop them...I rang Sea...Mr Keane as soon as I could.'

'Who's in charge here?' Murphy demanded.

'That would be me, sir.' DI Gowan responded as he approached. 'And you are?' he asked knowing full well who he was speaking with.

'I own the feckin place. And who gave *you* feckin permission to ransack *my* feckin club?' Murphy spit out.

'We have a warrant to search these premises, signed by my senior officer and an official of the Magistrates Court.' Gowan passed over the document.

Murphy snatched the paper from the DI and threw it to the floor. 'I don't give a feck about any feckin search warrant, just get the feck out of my club.' He pushed past the DI and tried to enter his office but was stopped by a uniformed officer.

'Sorry sir, I can't let you past,' said the officer, his arm barring Murphy's way.

'No one is stopping me going into my own office in my own club, least of all feckin you.' He grabbed the officer's arm and tried to drag him out of the way.

Dave Gowan stepped forward. 'Mr Murphy, if you continue to hamper the search of the premises I'll have to arrest you. Your choice, you can sit in the bar with a coffee while we continue with the business at hand or you can enjoy a cup of stale tea down at the station. What will it be? Murphy responded by pushing both officers out of the way and headed for the bar area.

'That went well,' Gowan said to the uniform.

'Not for long, sir,' he nodded towards the front door, Keane had arrived.

'Great, try and keep him out of my way will you, failing that arrest the both of them.' The DI went to see how Karina's forensic team were getting on in the cellar come store room, that was possibly the scene of the mutilations of Logan and Finch. Jonno stood watching through the open doorway. 'How's it going?' he asked as they watched two white coverall clad figures on their hands and knees looking for evidence that an actual crime had taken place.

'They've only really just got started,' replied Jonno.

'Karina, how long do you reckon on being?' Bad question.

Karina rose to the kneeling position and pulled the paper mask away from her face. 'Inspector, you of all people should know better than to ask such a bloody stupid question. It takes as long as it takes.'

'Ok, don't get stroppy, I'll leave you to it; I'm heading back to the nick. Let me know if they come up with anything, and keep your eye on those two out there.' Karina was still tutting to herself as he left.

***

The station canteen was near empty, the majority of the uniforms had eaten and returned to duty. Tanya sat having some quiet thinking time, poking and prodding with her fork at what was supposed to be a vegetarian lasagne, wondering how anything could be so bland. 'Here you are, hope you're not skiving?' said DS Jenny Bright as she walked across the canteen.

'Just grabbing my lunch while I can, sarge.'

'How's it going with skelly?' Jenny asked as she pulled out a chair and sat down.

'Looks like we've got a DNA match; it seems our pile of bones is the long lost father of the one and only, Sean Keane.'

'Well I never. That's two plusses, getting an ID and getting Keane's DNA on file, how on earth did you manage that.' This produced a smile from Tanya.

'To be honest I don't really know. Let's face it he obviously isn't as bright as he thinks. I'm quite pleased myself, got to give a bit of the credit to Lee though, he put in the work finding Mrs O'Hara. He almost went bog eyed sorting through the old paper files at MISPER.' Tanya continued sorting through the debris on her plate.

'Don't tell him that, his head won't get through the canteen doorway.' They both laughed. 'Are you going to eat that or just play with it?' Jenny said as Tanya pushed the food around her plate.

DCI Marlowe sat at his desk deep in thought, wondering how he could wade his way through the latest round of staff appraisals before the end of the week. A knock at the door drew his attention.

'Boss, we've got a major problem,' DS Jenny Bright said as she rushed into Marlowe's office throwing the door back on its hinges.

'Calm down, Jenny, what's going on?' Jenny didn't usually get ruffled.

'The ISO Quality people are carrying out an inventory of all the expensive stuff in the evidence lock-up...'

'And?' Marlowe sat forward, resting on his elbows.

'The package of heroin with Murphy's prints on...it's gone missing.'

'You are on very dangerous ground, Sergeant, if this is a wind-up.'

'Straight up, boss, no one claims to have signed it out.'

'It *was* in the safe?'

'I'll double check, but I've looked myself, if it was it's not there now.'

'Shit, shit, shit.' Marlowe grunted.' They'd had every opportunity to bring Murphy in earlier and he'd vetoed it. Someone would be for the high jump if it wasn't found, pronto! 'This has got to be a cock-up. It can't have gone far. Has it been sent down to Central?'

'Not according to any paperwork I've seen.'

'Things don't just go missing in a police station, especially from a secure room. There's got to be a trail, confirm that it was actually signed-in, check the signature in the log and see if the computer records match up. Double check dates, times, everything, before I have to report it to the Super and make myself look like an arse.'

'On my way,' Jenny turned on her heels.

'And I want to know who was supposed to be on duty in the lock-up when it went missing,' Marlowe called after her.

Marlowe's head was thumping, he tried to beat the semi-functioning coffee machine into submission with a couple of well aimed blows. The red light refused to turn green for go. The situation was beyond comprehension, how the hell could such a thing happen, there were enough procedures in place to ensure such an event never, ever happened. Coffee-less, Marlowe returned to his chair, still not fully grasping things he sat finger tapping on the veneer top of the desk, he picked up the telephone. 'Trevor, you got a minute,' he said into the handset only to be met with some petty excuse, 'I don't give a toss how busy you are, get your arse in here now,' and slammed down the receiver.

A minute later there was a knock at the door and not very happy Sergeant Trevor Cleeves walked in and sat down across from Marlowe. 'Hell fire, Columbo, what's so bleedin' important it couldn't wait until I'd finished my mug of tea?' The Sergeant sat without waiting to be asked.

'You're going to want something stronger than tea when I tell you. Murphy's drugs have gone missing.'

'Piss off.' Cleeves stood up to leave.

'Trevor, sit down. The ISO quality people or whoever they are, are doing an audit, and I'm telling you the package has gone missing.' Cleeves dropped back into the chair.

'I thought it was a wind up.' Cleeves slacked off his tie and ran his finger around the inside of his shirt collar, he was suddenly uncomfortably hot. 'I thought it was payback time.'

'Do I look as if I'm joking,' Marlowe said solemnly looking across to his friend.

'How could it happen? No point in asking if you're sure, I suppose?'

'Jenny's checked and double checked, I've got her looking into it. Thing is, it's your lot, uniform, who are responsible for the evidence lock-up'

'Now wait a bleedin' minute, if you're trying to lay the blame at my doorstep you've got another thing coming, SIR.' Being lifelong friends a question of rank had never been an issue between the two men, until now.

'Calm down, Trev, I'm not blaming anyone let alone you. But you see my point? there's a ninety-nine percent chance that a uniformed officer is involved.'

'And I'm going to find out who it is.' Cleeves responded sharply. 'How much was it worth anyway?'

'Only in the region of £80k plus.'

Cleeves gave a whistler. 'Fucking hell, I didn't realise.' He was getting hotter.

'You alright, Trev, you look like crap?' The change in Cleeves face hadn't gone un-noticed.

'Just a virus or something.' He lied, as he rubbed a hand across his chest.

'I don't know how long we can sit on this. Twenty four hours at a push before we…I have to let the Super know.'

'Right let's find it and the little sod who nicked it,' Cleeves once again stood up to leave.

'Trev, I'll let Dave Gowan know what's happening but apart from him let's keep it between us and Jenny until we know for certain what's going on.'

'Fair enough.' Cleeves left the office and stood in the corridor he could feel the sweat running down his back, his heart was beating far too fast and he didn't feel too good, *only indigestion* he thought.

Marlowe could see Cleeves outline through the glass panelled door. 'Sure you're alright out there, Trev?' he called.

'No worries, Phil,' he said and slipped away with the intention of finding Jenny, but not before he'd called Keane. Marlowe on the other hand looked again towards the coffee machine, swore and went in search of a caffeine and nicotine fix.

Karina the CSE was waiting when Marlowe returned. 'Now then, Karina, what can I do for you?'

'*The Snake Pit*, I've got some interesting information to share.' She passed over a slim manila file.

'Have I got to read this or are going to give me the abridged version?' asked the DCI.

'The search of the office and club produced nothing to speak about, just the odd trace of Cocaine on the back of a couple of toilet cisterns.'

'Nothing in the office?' he asked.

'Bugger all, we're still waiting for the result of samples we took from the store room, but I'm not holding my breath, it's been cleaned top to bottom. I've left Gary finishing off. However we did find this,' she placed a plastic test tube on the desk, in it was a tooth. 'Don't know who it belongs too yet though.'

'Logan, one would assume.'

'Yeah right, but we've still got to confirm it.' Karina didn't like assumptions.

'Ok, let me know when you do, and thanks.' Karina smiled and left.

Chapter 26

10.30pm that same evening, an attractive young couple joined the hustle and bustling crowd of young people waiting to get into the *Snake Pit*. Tanya, who always dressed conservatively for work was wearing a very short skirt and a thin strappy top. Like most of the young women in the queue, her outfit left very little to the imagination. Tanya set the ground rules for the evening. 'Lee, let's get this straight, I know we have to make this look realistic, but watch where you're putting your hands, if you don't want to go into the station in the morning with a black eye.' Lee laughed and put his arm around Tanya's shoulder as they moved up the line.

They eventually reached the font of the queue. 'Have you got some ID?' the doorman asked questioning Lee's age when they reached the club entrance. Angrily he produced his driving licence and they were allowed to enter. 'Well, I don't suppose you were expecting that? Tanya said laughing.

'No I bloody wasn't, wait 'till we raid the place and I arrest the sod.' She laughed again at his outburst.

They passed through the dimly lit foyer and went inside. The interior of the club was a dramatic contrast to the gloom of the daylight hours, now the glitter ball glittered, and the fairy lights twinkled. Tanya and Lee edged their way through the crowd and found a space at the bar.

'What do you want to drink?' Lee almost had to shout to make himself heard as they stood hemmed in.

'Lemon and lime, don't forget we're on duty,' Tanya said into his ear, leaning close for appearance sake.

'How can I forget? With you keep reminding me every ten minutes.' The undercover officers took their drinks and found a raised area away from where the crowds gathered in front of the DJ's stage. The remainder of the evening was spent drinking soft drinks and observing. On the surface things looked normal, just a young crowd enjoying a drink and the music. 'Not bad in here is it,' said Lee nodding his head and tapping his foot to the music.

'Oh shit,' said Tanya, spinning Lee around towards her and burying her face into his shoulder.

'I thought you said…' Lee was surprised at her actions.

'Don't be getting any ideas, I've just spotted Keane, don't forget I've already met him,' she said, sneaking a glance over Lee's shoulder. 'That was a close one.' Tanya freed herself from Lee's reluctant arms.

They watched Keane make his rounds of the dance floor, the fat bouncer never more than a couple of steps away. 'He's such a creep, look at him all touchy feely. Notice it's only the good looking girls without boyfriends he bothers with.' Tanya smiled, she couldn't help but notice a touch of envy in Lee's voice.

Keane continued his rounds, flirting with girls and giving a slap on the shoulder to various young men.

''Ello, 'ello,' said Lee, as they watched the fat bouncer leave Keane's side to disappear through a fire exit door, followed by one of the punters who returned on his own a couple of minutes later.

'What do you reckon's going on, doing a bit on the side?' Tanya asked.

'Yeah, but you'd think he'd be a bit more discreet.'

'No need to be discreet is there. It's not as if they know they have a couple of coppers watching them.'

'True,' Lee replied, 'ready for another drink yet?'

'No thanks, I'm alright for now.' Tanya picked up her drink.

'I haven't seen Murphy make an appearance, probably keeps out the way,' said Lee, watching the bouncer trading.

'That's if he's here at all. If it was me I wouldn't do the night shift, I'd leave it to the hired help.'

'Here we go again,' said Lee as the fat bouncer made his way towards the fire door. 'Think I'll take a walk over and see what's happening.'

'Don't do anything stupid, be careful.' She knew the words were wasted.

Lee shouldered his way across the dance floor. The bouncer returned to Keane's side before Lee reached the fire door. Tanya watched. Lee moved to the blind side of the door, watched the bouncer come out and waited to make sure he wasn't going to do an about turn. The bouncer moved from view onto the dance floor, Lee waited a couple of minutes then checked over his shoulder, opened the door and then disappeared closing the door behind him.

Tanya's heart almost leapt into her mouth, both Keane and the bouncer stopped dead on the dance floor, heads close together as words were exchanged and then they did an about turn, making for the exit. Lee was still on the opposite side of the door when Keane and the bouncer entered the passageway.

Tanya immediately put down her glass and shoved her way through the dancers, she reached the fire exit, stood and waited but Lee never returned. She grabbed the door handle and tried to open it, it had been locked from the other side. There was very little Tanya could do but watch the clock and wait. In the reasonable quiet of the ladies toilet she took the mobile from her bag and dialled.

'Are you sure he just hasn't got fixed up and gone off with some girl?' DI Gowan said down the phone.

'Sir, I know he can be a prick at times but seriously, I'm sure something's happened to him.' Tanya said making the call from the cloakroom.

'Ok, I'm on my way, go outside and wait, I shouldn't be too long.' Tanya stood outside the club. Shivering she wrapped her arms around herself as she waited.

***

Once he was sure he wouldn't be interrupted, Lee closed the fire exit door behind him as he entered a short passage way. A further two doors were ahead of him, one the emergency exit into the car park, the other signed Manager. Lee put his ear to the manager's door, no sound came from inside, he put his hand on the door knob and slowly turned, still no sound as the door opened slightly. 'Well, well, well, what have we got here?' Keane said. Deep in concentration he hadn't heard Keane and the fat bouncer enter the passageway and close the door behind them. Lee froze to the spot he knew he didn't stand a chance of talking his way out of the situation.

'You do know you're not supposed to be in here?'

'Yeah sorry, thought the gents was this way.' Lee tried to edge his way past the bouncer.

'Yeah right...not so fast.' Keane grabbed Lee's arm above the elbow. 'What the fuck was you hoping to find in there?' he gestured towards the office. Lee stood his ground and tried to shrug off the hand gripping his bicep.

'Nowt to say?' the fat bouncer said as he grabbed Lee by the front of his shirt and slammed him into the wall knocking the wind out of him. Not that Lee was in a position to say anything. He gasped for breath when the bouncer roughly placed his forearm under his chin and across his throat, cutting off his breath. Feebly Lee struggled to free himself as Keane searched his pockets.

'Steady up, pal.' Keane reached around and took Lee's wallet from his back trouser pocket. 'What's this?' he said as Lee's warrant card fell to the floor. 'Look what we've got here, a piglet.' Keane picked up the warrant card. They both laughed and began making snorting pig noises, all the while Lee gasped for breath.

The bouncer released the pressure. Lee brought his hands to his face, coughing and spluttering, then, wham, a fist struck the young DC in the solar plexus. Lee collapsed to the floor.

'What the fuck we gonna do now? The fat bouncer asked Keane.

'Give me a minute, need to think.'

'You'd better think fast,' said the bouncer, 'he might have mates out there.'

146

'Shut up you tart, the doors locked nobody's coming through here. Give us a hand.' Both men bent forward and hoisted Lee from the floor. The young cop started to hyperventilate as panic set in, his eyes rolled in his head and his body went limp, hanging on the bouncers arm. 'Now look what' you've done, you've fucking killed him.'

'Don't be daft, he's just passed out. What are we going to do with him anyway?'

'I think Uncle Pat might want to have a word, get him out the door and shove him in the boot of the car.'

***

Tanya kept looking at her watch, hoping that Dave Gowan would get his finger out. She started pacing up and down half expecting a squad car to turn up any minute, a few minutes later the DIs Audi pulled into the kerb side. He was alone. Tanya walked over and climbed in the passenger side, pleased to get warmed up.

'Alright, Tanya?'

'You're on your own?' Tanya sounded desperate.

'Could hardly bring half the station with me could I, especially if he's gone off on the pull. Come on then, fill me in on what's happened.'

'Not much really, it was obvious there was dealing going on, well, Lee being Lee, said he was going to check it out. Anyway, no sooner had he sneaked through the emergency exit when Keane and his shadow decided to do the same. That was the last I saw of him, then I called you.'

'Come on, show me what's what.'

Tanya left the warmth of the Audi and led the DI into the club foyer.

'Budge over lads,' Gowan said to a group of young men waiting to be admitted into the club.

'Piss off, get to the back of the queue,' they all echoed. Things changed once the DI produced his identification.

'I want a word with the manager,' Gowan demanded to a surly looking doorman.

'Can I ask what about?' A big fella in a dark suit asked.

'No, just get the manager,' was the only response from Gowan.

The door man shrugged his shoulders and shuffled off on muscular legs that rubbed together, Gowan winced as he watched him walk away. Five minutes later he returned, following behind a skinny man, about five feet six inches tall with spiky hair and a spotty face. The young man didn't look old enough to be in the club, never mind being in charge.

'Officer, madam, my name's James, I'm the assistant manager how can I help you?'

'I'd rather have a word with Mr Keane,' said Gowan firmly.

'I'm sorry Mr Keane isn't on the premises, you'll have to make do with me I'm afraid.'

You will be afraid in a minute you pompous little git, Gowan thought to himself.

'This young lady came to the club with her boyfriend and now she believes he's gone missing.' He gestured towards Tanya. 'I'd like to come in and have a look around if that's ok.' Gowan omitted the fact that Tanya and Lee were police officers.

Showing bravado in front of the door staff the spotty youth asked. 'Do you have a search warrant?'

'Do I need one? Because it can be arranged, only I'll have to shut you down until it's sorted.' Gowan looked to Tanya and some kind of subliminal message passed between them.

'Be my guest, allow me to show you around,' he stepped to one side allowing Gowan and Tanya to enter, the doorman stayed where he was blocking their way.

Gowan stopped dead in his tracks in front of the defiant looking doorman who was still partially blocked their way. Gowan invaded the man's personal space, almost nose to nose in a staring match. The doorman blinked and moved aside. They moved through the crowded foyer into the gloom and flashing lights of the club. Closely followed by spotty youth and the doorman, Tanya led the way to the fire exit door she'd watched Lee disappear through. Dave Gowan was just about to put his hand on the handle.

'You can't go in there,' said Spotty putting out his hand to stop Gowan, he smiled. 'If you open it, you'll set the alarms off.' Gowan raised his eyebrows, firmly grabbed a hold of the door handle and turned, the door opened. No alarm.

'You were saying?' Gowan said as he opened the door. There wasn't much to see beyond the door, a narrow passage way with chipped magnolia painted walls, two further doors led off the passage, one to the manager's office and the other leading into the car park. Gowan opened both, no sign of DC Kristianson. To put the "young lady's" mind at ease, Gowan insisted they be shown the remaining rooms in the club, still there was nothing to reveal Lee had been there. A quick inspection of the car park also proved to be negative.

Spotty smiled, shrugged his shoulders and escorted Gowan and Tanya back to the foyer. 'Sorry we couldn't help you, officer. I'm sure your boyfriend will turn up sooner or later,' he said turning to Tanya and then walked away leaving the doorman to show them out.

'Well, what do we do now?' asked Tanya when they were back outside.

'There's no evidence of anything going on here, and there's always the chance he could have gone off with some girl.'

'There's only one person he's gone off with and that's Sean Keane,' Tanya protested.

'That's as may be, but for now we go back to the nick and get uniform to keep an eye out, and if he hasn't turned up by morning we'll have to think again. Come on, get in,' he held the door of the Audi open. He couldn't stop himself from taking a sneaky glance at Tanya's legs as she climbed in.

'Sean I can't believe just how feckin brainless you are.' Murphy stood with his back to the patio doors. 'And I don't know why you're looking so feckin smug, you fat bastard.' Both Keane and Fatty stood before Murphy like a couple of school boys in front of the headmaster, not like the hard men they were.

'Look at it from our point of view, Uncle Pat, if we hadn't stopped him when we did he'd have been all over the office and what then?' Keane blustered out.

'You could have just *asked* him to *leave*, and we wouldn't be in this feckin mess, you feckin idiots.'

'Yeah…well we got a bit carried away, anyhow it's too late now what shall we do with him?' asked Keane not daring to look his uncle in the eye.

'What shall *we* do with him…you have the feckin nerve to ask *me* that?'

'I'm asking for help, Uncle Pat.'

'Where is he now?' Murphy questioned.

'In the boot of the car,' the bouncer chipped in then laughed.

'This get's feckin worse by the feckin minute. Still alive?'

'He was the last time I checked,' replied Keane.

'Well that's a feckin shame, get him in the stable out of the way.' Murphy couldn't believe his nephew's stupidity, it seemed to be one problem after another.

Chapter 27

It was virtually standing room only as Tanya, Gowan and Jenny gathered in the DCI's office for an impromptu meeting.

'For Christ's sake, Tanya, I knew it was a bad move. What did I tell you? *Be careful* that's what I bloody said, and what happened? You went and bloody lost your partner.'

'To be fair, boss, it was hardly Tanya's fault if the silly bugger decided to go off playing the *Lone Ranger*, is it?' DI Gowan interjected.

'You're as bloody bad, inspector, you should have got things on the move last night. Have uniform reported anything?' Marlowe stood and started pacing around the small office.

'Not a word, they kept a discreet eye on the club until well after closing time.' Gowan replied.

'Has anyone been around to his home?' Marlowe continued pacing.

'I rang his mum before I came in. She checked his room and said it doesn't look like he's been home.' Tanya said, concerned.

'This is turning into a bloody farce, first the drugs in the lock-up disappear and now Lee.' Tanya looked from Marlowe to Gowan and back again, this was the first she'd heard about the missing drugs. 'Yes, Tanya,' Marlowe said before she had a chance to open her mouth, 'the package with Murphy's prints has been nicked right from under our noses. A bloody farce.'

'What are we going to do, boss?' asked DS Bright.

'Get to the bloody bottom of this and find our young copper, quick. Ok, officially time to get worried. What else do we know, Jenny?'

'After, Karina left the club yesterday, Gary, one of her team thought he'd try spraying some luminal about the place and it paid off, it showed large blood patches on the floor, despite the dowsing down with bleach.' Jenny told them.

'How did they explain it?' asked the DCI.

'Straight forward, they reckoned one of the barmen slipped and sliced his arm on a broken bottle. Had the spiel off to pat, even had a bloke with a bandage on his arm.' Gowan added, finding his voice again after his bollocking

'That it?'

'Yep, nothing more to report.'

'What about Keane? Is there any more intel on him?' asked Marlowe.

'Haven't had a chance to tell you, boss. We got the results of Keane's DNA test back, he's definitely related to the skelly from the toilet,' Tanya divulged.

'Bet you a pound to a penny Murphy's tied up in it somewhere as well. Right, our priority as of now is to find our missing copper. Jenny get a hold of Jonno, I want another search of the club, top to bottom and get the CCTV checked, see if it picks up Keane's vehicle leaving the club.'

'Right, boss.' Jenny left the office with Tanya close behind.

'Dave, there's no point messing about, let's bring Keane and his fat friend Conway in.' Marlowe glanced at the clock on the wall, it was 9.15am. 'The times hardly ideal but I should imagine they're both still tucked up in bed and won't be expecting a pull. So let's get our arses into gear and bring them in.' Marlowe had a preference for making "house calls" on the unsuspecting at the crack of dawn, a time when it was least expected and those favoured had their guards down.

'What about, Murphy?' asked Dave Gowan.

'Best leave him be, at least until the missing drugs turn up. I'll take a team and drag Keane out of his pit.'

'Suppose that leaves me with his fat mate then.'

'Better take a couple of Cleeves' big lads with you just in case he gets stroppy.' Marlowe smiled, he was long past the stage of tussling with overweight villains.

'Thanks for that, boss.'

'Tell Tanya, she's with me will you?' Gowan was just about to leave the office. 'And I want that bloody club searched yet again, and I want something found this time.'

While the teams were assembled, Marlowe took the opportunity of an impromptu smoke break, *where the hell had Lee disappeared to*? He kept asking himself, making the promise to return him to uniform if he had indeed gone off with some young woman, but in the back of his mind he knew it was wishful thinking. The lad was in trouble.

Sean Keane lived on Hull's regenerated Victoria Dock complex in the east of the city, once a working dock it was now the height of sophistication. Keane's apartment was on the river front, a third floor overlooking the River Humber, not quite the Mediterranean but an impressive view all the same. At 9.45am Marlowe and his team pulled up in the apartment car park. DCI Marlowe along with Tanya was in the lead vehicle and four uniformed officers in the following vehicle made up the team. Hoping time was still on their side, Marlowe issued instructions to the waiting officers.

'Ok, just to be on the safe side I want you two to cover the stairs, you never know if he decides to do a runner,' Marlowe told the nearest uniforms. 'You two come with us.' At the rear entrance to the apartment block Marlowe pressed the intercom button marked deliveries. A quick show of IDs to the caretaker and they were in the building. Once inside the building, the uniforms placed themselves at the stairwell. The remaining two uniforms and Tanya followed the DCI. The caretaker led them through a series of corridors to the foyer. A further luxurious carpeted hallway led them to the lift and up to the third floor. 'You ready for this?' Marlowe asked the DC as they approached Keane's door. She nodded. 'Go on then.'

Marlowe stood to one side of the door, Tanya put a finger to the doorbell and pressed, they could hear the bell shrilling inside, no answer. Tanya looked towards Marlowe and pressed again, this time for an extended period then hammered with her fist on the wooded door.

'Hang on, give me a minute will you, I heard you the first time,' an irritated voice called out. On the other side of the door they heard the safety chain removed, a key turned and the door was opened. Keane stood before them wearing nothing but his boxer shorts. 'DC Etherington, how nice to see you,' Keane said sarcastically.

Marlowe stepped into view. 'Good morning, Mr Keane, hope we haven't got you out of bed.'

'Bloody hell, what do you two want?' Keane put his hand down his shorts and made a show of scratching.

'We'd like you to come down to the station to answer a few questions,' replied Tanya.

'Well you'll just have to want on, I'm going back to bed.' He grabbed the door to slam it shut. Marlowe's foot prevented the door closing.

'Are you going to move it or what?' asked Keane as the door bounced back at him.

'Or what,' said Marlowe as he pushed his way into the apartment. 'Get dressed, or you can come as you are. Your choice.'

'Oh, what the hell,' he said as the uniformed officers edged their way into the apartment.

Keane turned his back and walked to the bedroom to dress. 'Do you mind?' he said as Tanya followed and prevented him closing the bedroom door.

'Not if you don't,' not going anywhere she stood sideways in the doorway. *So this is how the other half live*, she thought as she looked through into the lounge where the DCI was making a very quick and impromptu search while Keane was occupied.

'Have we time for a coffee before you cart me down to the nick?' Keane asked.

'Why don't you have a couple of slices of toast while you're at it? Marlowe called out sarcastically from the living room, where he now sat with his feet up, looking through a motoring magazine. 'Just hurry up will you.'

'Are you going to tell me what all this is about,' Keane asked as he pushed past Tanya and went into the living room. 'Do you mind taking your feet off the coffee table? Cost a lot of money that.' Marlowe smiled and did as he was asked.

'And very nice too. Did you get a loan from Kwik Kash to pay for it?' The quick response surprised Marlowe himself. 'And yes, I'll tell you what it's all about – when we get to the station.

'I take it I'm not under arrest?'

'Questions, questions, questions, Mr Keane, no you are not under arrest, but if you take much bloody longer I'll find something to arrest you for. I'm sure we'd find something in the flat if we look hard enough. Now if you're ready? Or shall I ask the lads downstairs to come and give you a hand?'

Keane reluctantly left the apartment, locked the door and sandwiched between Marlowe and Tanya they headed for the vehicles in the car park. 'Mind your head,' said a unformed constable, as he tried to prevent Keane's head banging on the door pillar as he helped him into the rear seats of the squad car.

'Off, do *not* touch me,' Keane shrugged him away and in the process his head bounced off the metal to a round of sniggering. 'And I won't be saying a word until I've seen my brief,' he rubbed vigorously at his head.

Back at the station Keane was duly processed. 'Now wait a friggin minute, what's the game? I haven't been charged so why the hell are you banging me up?' the officer didn't answer, and escorted him to a cell. He pushed Keane inside and slammed the door. 'I know my fucking rights,' he called out to no avail.

***

Unfortunately for Sergeant Trevor Cleeves, he was on duty in the custody suite as Keane arrived. Cleeves paled when saw

Keane ushered in and made to stand before the custody desk and empty his pockets. Try as he might Cleeves couldn't avoid eye contact as he booked him into the system. Keane stood as if he didn't have a care in the world. After all he had every confidence that his very expensive lawyer would get him out of the place before the club opened.

Keane was led away to a holding cell to await his brief and the oncoming interview. Cleeves physically shook as he tried to finish the paperwork, cold sweat came over him and the *indigestion* returned.

'Give us that, sarge,' his junior colleague said and took the pen out of Cleeves shaking hand. 'You look like crap, why don't you go get yourself a mug of tea while I finish off?'

'Yeah, thanks I think I will.'

Cleeves went through to the back office and with shaking hands made himself a fresh mug of tea. Holding onto the worktop he felt considerably worse. 'You alright back there, sarge?'

Cleeves' chest felt tight, constricted as if a thick rubber band was squashing the life out of him. 'I'm not feeling too good, Stan.'

Stan, his junior colleague came through to the back office, he was shocked at what he saw. Cleeves was still standing at the worktop, gripping with all his might, his face ashen. 'Sod this, sarge,' he helped Cleeves to a chair. 'This is the Gordon Street Police Station, we need an ambulance, quick…' he said into the telephone.

***

Keane had been the last person the Sergeant was expecting to be escorted into the station. He'd managed to remove the package from the safe in secure evidence lock-up without incurring any problems, after all he had they keys. Using the log-on details belonging to a colleague on long term sick leave he accessed the evidence log on the computer system and erased the details and the page in the written log was misplaced. Cleeves was sure he couldn't have covered his tracks any better. It had been relatively easy to implicate an unpopular colleague, especially one who already had various doubts against his character.

Cleeves knew it wasn't in Keane's interest to make their association known. Keane would keep his mouth shut. It was the fact that in all his years in the force this was the first time he'd crossed the line. He didn't want the world to know about his junkie son and with retirement looming a few short months away he had thought the risk was one worth taking, the opportunity to fill the coffers for a rainy day. Now he was wishing he had never agreed to meet Keane that evening.

***

Marlowe was reinstated behind his desk when there was a knock on the door and it opened immediately. There was only one person who'd take the liberty of walking straight in. 'Trevor, I hope you haven't come to waste my time...sorry, Stan,' Marlowe said as he looked up. 'I was expecting it to be your Sergeant.'

'That's what I've come about; he's just been carted off in an ambulance. It looks like he's had a heart attack.'

'Bloody hell, the poor old bugger. To tell the truth he looked ill earlier on, said it was indigestion.'

'I'll let you know when I hear from the hospital, sir.'

'Cheers, Stan, I'd appreciate that.'

'No problem, sir.' Then he was gone, closing the door behind him.

Marlowe, still sitting behind his desk suddenly felt old. He was only a year or two younger than his old friend. It made him wonder, it could happen to anyone at anytime. Then there was a knock on the door, again. This time it was his DI.

'Bloody hell what happened to you?' Gowan came in sporting a bruise to the right side of his face.

'Need you *really* ask?' Gowan said as he wearily dropped down onto the DCIs office sofa. 'You want to see some of the other lads.'

'Conway, the bouncer?'

'Bloody right it was. I'll tell you what, he may be a fat sod but he's a scrapper. Robbo, the big lad from uniform, he took a nasty blow to his neck. We had to take him to the infirmary.'

'That bad?' asked Marlowe.

'Well, not very good if I'm being honest.'

'Did you tell Conway why he was brought in?'

'He didn't give us a chance. Just went bonkers when Jonno told him to get his fat arse into gear. All I can say is he must be a very sensitive bloke 'cos he went ballistic. That was when he clobbered, Robbo, so I arrested the fat twat.'

Marlowe stood up from his desk, walked across to his malfunctioning coffee machine and gave it a thump, the red light refused to turn green as he knew it would. 'Come on, let's grab a coffee in the canteen while we wait for their brief to turn up. I suppose they're sharing Murphy's lawyer, Brigham?' Marlowe held the door open.

'Yeah, Mr Plastic,' said Gowan, 'by the way, those animal hairs found on the body parts were horse hairs.'

'And do we know anyone who keeps horses?'

'There's not very many riding stables along Hessle Road,' came the sarcastic reply. 'I'll ask around.'

'By the way, have you heard about Cleevsey?' Marlowe asked. 'Silly old buggers only gone and had a heart attack.'

Chapter 28

Lee didn't know how long he'd been in the stable. It could have been hours or days. Time was something he couldn't get to grips with. He did know he was hungry and thirsty. On his arrival at the stable he had received a battering from the fat bouncer that had left him bruised and aching. The fuzzy feeling in his head made him wonder if he'd been given something else apart from a beating. The sound of feet crunching on gravel roused Lee from what he thought could be a drug induced daze.

Lee filled the space once occupied by the deceased Anderson. The young detective lay amongst the bales of hay, ankles and hands fixed fast with plastic ties, and a dirty rag stuffed in his mouth didn't help matters. The key turned in the lock. Lee looked through tired eyes as Murphy entered the stable.

'Well, young fella, what the feck am I going to do with you?' Murphy said as he locked the door behind him and walked across to where the young detective lay. He took a draw on his miniature cigar and blew the smoke up into the timber beamed roof space. Murphy despaired of his nephew, *as if there wasn't enough shit happening at the minute.* Murphy sat down on a bale of hay and carried on with the one-sided conversation. 'If only you'd kept your feckin neb out of it, you wouldn't be in the shit and I wouldn't be having to sort it out.' Murphy stubbed out the cigar butt carefully on the concrete floor. 'You thirsty?' Lee nodded as vigorously as he could. Murphy reached for the plastic bottle of water by his side, still in pain from his own beating he hobbled across and pulled the rag from Lee's mouth.

'Mr Murphy, you've got to let me go...' Murphy didn't want to hear it and pushed the bottle neck into Lee's mouth, he drank thirstily until the liquid made him cough and ran down his chin.

'Feel better, lad?' Lee nodded and the rag was shoved back in before the young detective could plead his case further. 'I'll be back when I've decided what we're going to do with you.' There weren't many options available, barring one.

Chapter 29

'DC Etherington, I didn't expect we'd be meeting again so soon,' Keane said across the interview room table top. His Solicitor gave him one of those, "keep your gob shut" type of looks. 'And who have we got here?' he said looking at Jenny, pouting his lips.

'I'm Detective Sergeant Jenny Bright, and before we go any further we're obliged to read you your rights.'

'Oh please, spare me the formalities I've got a business to get on with.'

'Nevertheless, needs must,' said Jenny.

'Mr Keane I would like to point out that both an audio tape and a video recording of this interview are being made,' she pointed to the flashing red light on the camera high in the corner of the room. Tanya un-wrapped two cassette tapes and placed them in the twin recorder. 'The time is 2.45pm, present are Mr Sean Keane, Mr Graham Brigham, DS Jenny Bright and DC Tanya Etherington.' Jenny proceeded to issue the formal caution. 'You do not have to say anything. But it may harm your defence if you do not mention when questioned something which you later rely on in court. Anything you do say may be given in evidence.'

'Right, now that's out of the way can we please get on with things?' Keane sat back in his chair trying to look as if he didn't have a care in the world.

Brigham, with his spectacles resting on the end of his nose, sat with pen poised over his notepad. 'Shall we commence?'

'Mr Keane, I believe you already know my colleague, DC Etherington?'

'Yes I have had the pleasure.' Keane blew Tanya an exaggerated kiss and winked.

Oh, you cocky bugger, thought Jenny. 'Mr Keane where were you on the evening of the 5th August?'

'That was Thursday, right? I was at the *Snake Pit*, working.'

'You were there all night?'

'Yup, busy night, I had my hands full.'

Tanya produced a monochrome photograph of Lee from the folder in front of her. Jenny spun it around and slid it across the table. 'Did you see this man in the club?'

Keane gave the picture a quick glance. 'No, never seen him.'

'You sure about that?' asked Jenny. 'I know for a fact he was in your club on Thursday night.'

'Then why are you asking the question of my client?' Brigham questioned.

'I'm merely stating that the man in the picture was in the club, what I want to know is does your client recall seeing him.'

'Oh come on, the place was heaving. I can't remember everyone who was in there, it's impossible.' Now he knew what it was all about he'd have to be cagey with his answer.

'Is that a yes or a no, Mr Keane?' asked Jenny.

'Then it's a no, I've never seen him before.'

'Where you at the club all night?'

'Of course I was, I run the place.'

'Can anyone vouch for you?'

'Anyone who was working that night will tell you I was there.' *I bet they will* she almost said out aloud.

'Well, now this is where its starts to get a bit complicated. We have a witness statement confirming the man *was* in the club, the trouble is he never left. Your own security camera shows him entering the club, and also confirms he never left.'

'So?' Keane showed no emotion in his face.

'So, the man in the photograph was seen to go through the emergency exit door.'

'There's your answer then, he exited,' Keane laughed.

'Logical, but not quite what we believe happened. You and your colleague were seen to follow the man through the door leading to the office, less than two minutes later.'

'And you do know that exit also leads to the car park. We often get people trying to sneak out for a smoke.' He smiled, full of confidence.

Jenny tapped the photograph with her finger. 'So you never saw him when you entered the corridor?'

'No, no one. Like I said he must have gone into the car park through the fire exit. Once outside, if the door closes behind you there's no way you can get back in. So if he went through there, no I wouldn't have seen him.' He was on a roll.

'We found his finger prints on the two interior doors, not the one leading to the car park. Any idea how they could have got there?' Keane shrugged his shoulders.

'Are we done here? This is getting us nowhere,' asked Brigham who so far had hardly said a word.

'Nearly, you said you never left the club until closing time, correct?' Tanya looked up from the note taking. She wanted to see the reaction from Keane.

'Let me think, I might have stepped out for a few minutes.'

'Where did you go in those few minutes?' asked Jenny.

'The kebab shop around the corner, I was starving. You can ask them, they know me in there.' *Shit*, thought Jenny more people taking a back hander.

Jenny was about to bring the meeting to a close and looked to Tanya. 'How did you feel about finding out about your father, Mr Keane,' asked Tanya.

Brigham looked surprised. 'Do I need to have a word with my client, detective?'

'No, not at all. I don't think Mr Keane minds me asking the question.' Brigham looked to his client who nodded agreement.

'Alright I suppose. At least now I know what happened, Ma's happier now that she knows he didn't just run off.'

'I don't suppose you can throw any light as to why he was digging a tunnel into the Midland Bank?' Tanya questioned.

'Are you stupid or just pretending? He wasn't trying to make a deposit now was he?'

'Detective, you said there was no need for me to discuss this with my client, well I think otherwise. I think we're finished here?'

'Just one more thing,' said Jenny, 'The evidence suggests your father didn't die due to the tunnel caving in, as we originally thought. He was murdered.'

Keane sat silent trying to take in what he'd been told. Visibly shaken, his thoughts were suddenly a million miles away. Murdered, surely there must be a mistake...an accident it had to be, and who the hell had he been carrying out the bank job with? There was only one person Keane knew who would have the balls to try and rob a bank, his Uncle Pat.

Chapter 30

'Jenny, I'm going to have a go at Gary Conway, you coming?' Dave Gowan said as he walked into the squad room.

'Hang on a mo while I just finish off.' Jenny clicked the mouse, closing the computer programme she'd been working on. She reached across her desk and picked up her A4 notebook. 'I hope we have better luck with Conway than we did with Keane. That was a right waste of time I tell you. Mind you, I did put the cat amongst the pigeons when I told him it looked like his old man had been topped.'

'How did he take it?' Gowan asked, smiling.

'He looked as if he could have been knocked over with a feather; I thought he was going to fall off his chair.' They both laughed.

'Anyway, I think we'll stand a much better chance with this one, he's not as bright as Keane and we've already got him for assault and grievous bodily harm.' Gowan put his finger to his eye which was starting to colour up where the bouncer had caught him with a right hook.

'Ouch,' said Jenny.

'Not me, I mean for the GBH on Robbo, they're keeping him in the Infirmary overnight.'

'Is he in a bad way?' Jenny asked concerned.

'No not really, it's just for observation to be on the safe side. He's as tough as old boots, he'll be as right as rain in the morning, bragging to anyone who'll listen.'

It wasn't a pretty sight when they walked into the interview room. Beside Brigham the plastic faced lawyer sat Conway, the fat bouncer. Conway looked worse for wear, his arse was hanging out of his ripped tight fitting jeans and his tee-shirt was almost in rags. Dave Gowan wasn't the only one wearing his wounds on show. The fat bouncer also had one or two bruises forming on his face from the earlier skirmish.

The formalities done with and Conway informed of his rights, the interview began proper.

'You do know why you are here, don't you, Mr Conway?' Dave Gowan asked as he leaned forward across the table.

''Course, smacking you and that other copper. Why else?'

'Why else indeed,' challenged Brigham, Conway's lawyer.

'We'll get to that in a minute, first of all, Mr Conway let me remind you, you have been arrested on two counts of GBH.'

'Yes, and my client pleads guilty to those charges, but at the same time claims that he was provoked into a violent situation by yourself and your officers.'

'That is debatable, Mr Brigham, but as I have a personal interest in that one,' Gowan touched the side of his injured face. 'I think it best if I leave it for one of my colleagues to discuss with your client later.'

'As you wish, inspector,' Brigham replied through his barely moving lips.

Dave Gowan made a show of pretending to study the information in the folder that lay opened on the table and looked up. 'Ian Anderson, Chas Logan and John Finch, I take it that you know these men?'

'The names ring a bell, can't say much else.' He looked up at the blinking red light on the video camera, high in a corner pointing towards him.

'And, Mr Conway are you in anyway associated with the owner of the *Snake Pit*, Mr Patrick Murphy and his nephew Sean Keane?' asked Gowan.

'Yeah, I work for them.' The fat bouncer was looking down at his hands, picking the dried skin from around his finger nails and letting the bits fall to the floor.

'You work the door?'

'Amongst other things.' He brought a hand to his mouth again, biting at the already bitten to the quick nails.

'Such as?'

'I'm Sean…Mr Keane's right-hand man.' He spat a piece of nail on the carpet. Until now Jenny had been concentrating on her note book, the remark made her look up and smile.

'By right-hand man, you mean you beat to a pulp anyone Mr Keane tells you to. Even go as far as cutting their ears off or ripping the tongues out of their mouths?'

'Whoa, hang on a minute…' Conway stammered and was cut short by his lawyer.

'My client has the right to remain silent,' said Brigham as he stuck an elbow into Conway's ribs.

'No comment,' came from the mouth of the fat bouncer.

'Not even about the dismembered body of Ian Anderson, you've nothing to say about that?'

'No comment,' Conway shifted uneasy in his seat.

'Officers, please ask a direct question.'

'Were you at the Snake Pit on the evening of 5th August?' asked Gowan.

''Course I was. I was working that night.'

'Did you see this man during the course of the evening?' Gowan produced a photograph of DC Kristianson from the folder and slid it across the table. 'Before you answer, think very carefully what you're going to say.' Gowan knew he'd struck a nerve, sweat started to glisten on Conway's forehead and the muscles in his neck visibly tightened as he looked at the picture.

Conway looked to his lawyer, he raised his eyebrows in response. 'No comment.'

'Are you sure, Mr Conway? The reason I ask if you're sure is because this man is missing, and what's more he's a serving police officer who was last seen in the *Snake Pit* on the night in question.'

'No comment.' Conway squirmed in his seat.

'Well if that's all, gentlemen?' Brigham made ready to leave.'

'Yes, that'll do for now, thank you, Mr Brigham.'

'And my client, he's free to leave?' The lawyer asked.

'Unfortunately not just yet I'm afraid. Your client still has to face the GBH charge.'

'A word with my client before I leave - in private?'

'Of course,' said Gowan, who formally terminated the interview, leaving Conway and Brigham alone in the interview room.

'I bet you ten quid Brigham's now telling Fatty to keep his gob well and truly shut,' said Jenny when they were back in the corridor.

'Sorry, Jenny I'm not taking you up on that, no matter what odds you're offering.' Gowan turned. 'Take him back to his cell when his lawyer comes out,' he instructed the uniform standing on sentry duty outside of the interview room. 'Let's grab a coffee and see if there's been any sighting of young Lee.'

***

Keane hadn't heard anything from Conway, or Brigham the plastic faced brief. The best he could hope for was that Fatty was playing it cagey and keeping his mouth well and truly shut.

'So, lad, how did it go?' Murphy asked his nephew.

'So, so, Uncle Pat.' His thoughts kept returning to what the police had told him. Thoughts he was keeping to himself, for the time being. He was sure the opportunity to bring it up wasn't far away.

'Good lad. What about Anderson, any mention?'

'It did come up in conversation, Uncle Pat.' Both men laughed, one haughtier than the other.

'Keep 'em guessing, tell 'em feck all.'

Keane and Murphy had been steadily drinking for the past hour and a half. The whisky decanter was now down below the plimsoll line. The air in the study was heavy with cigar and cigarette smoke, which hovered in a blue cloud below the ceiling. Keane had other things on his mind, he studied his uncle's face, looking for a sign, anything. The mood of both men was heavy with nostalgia about the old days, more precisely Keane's childhood.

The whisky had started to give Keane that *I don't give a toss and sod the consequences feeling*. 'Tell me about my dad, Uncle Pat. Why do you put him down all the time, he can't have been all bad, surely?' Keane's brow furrowed as he waited for an answer.

'Because he was a tosser, son. ' He stood up from the easy chair, wincing at the pain in his ribs as he crossed to the table. Picking up his miniature cigars, he took one out of the packet and lit up. 'A tosser of the first order, always was, and he would be today if he was here now,' he said exhaling a plume of smoke. His body ached as he walked across to the French doors and opened them. The hit of fresh air made him wobble slightly on unsteady legs. He looked down the paddock towards the stables to where their guest was trussed up. He shook his head, *another mess to clear up.*

'I know I never knew the bloke, but you tell a different story to, Ma. She reckoned deep down that something bad must have happened to him, that he'd never have deserted her when she was having me.'

Murphy turned facing into the room. 'Leave it, son. You were better off without him, you and your Ma. He was no good, a chancer and loser just like Logan, Finch and that wanker Anderson. He'd never have made anything of himself.' He put his cigar to his lips, it was dead. He threw the butt into the fireplace.

The whisky was also taking its toll on Keane. Outwardly he looked calm and relaxed but inside his brain was in overdrive, he needed to know. He had no intention of letting the subject rest. 'He might have made something of himself if you'd taken an interest, helped him, like.' The cigarette hung from his lips, eyes squinting through the smoke as he spoke.

'Help him? Believe me, son, I tried my feckin best for your Ma's sake. No matter how hard I tried I couldn't take to him. Always acting the big man he was, wanting more and more. I was glad when he feckin died.'

'Did you say *died*?' Keane was out of his chair and on his feet facing the older man.

'Slip of the tongue, lad, I mean I'm glad the bastard is dead.' Murphy was cursing himself for taking his eye of the ball and letting the whisky do his talking.

'You definitely said, "when he feckin died",' Keane pointed accusingly at his Uncle with an outstretched arm, '"died" you said.'

'It's just the booze talking. I never hid the fact that I didn't like him, when he disappeared I hoped the fecker was dead, just the booze talking, mixing my words up. Here, pass me your glass and I'll top it up.' Murphy hoped he'd said enough to calm his nephew down.

Keane passed across his glass. Whisky in hand he returned to his chair and sat down. The mood was tense following the outburst. Murphy remained standing, swaying slightly with the effects of the alcohol. Keane leaned back in the armchair nursing his glass with both hands. He turned his head and stared out of the window, thinking of his uncle's words.

Unable to leave it alone, he faced the old man once again. 'You knew he was dead didn't you? All these years and you let Ma think he'd pissed off and left us. How could you do that to your own sister?' Murphy remained quiet. Lost for words as the past came back to taunt him. 'It wouldn't surprise me if it was you who'd killed him.' The change in Murphy's face became a pained expression, one that Keane couldn't help but notice. 'You did it, didn't you…you killed my dad?'

Murphy knew that maybe the past would catch up with him, but not like this. He loved Keane like he was his own son. 'It was a long time ago, lad, an accident.'

'Accident! If it was an accident why didn't you tell, Ma?' Keane's voice was starting to rise.

'Let me explain...' Murphy protested.

'How can you explain murdering your own sister's husband?' Keane was back on his feet, his face close enough his uncle's to smell the whisky and stale cigars.

Murphy stepped back. 'It wasn't like that ... we were on a job, a bank job.'

'I fucking knew it, soon as the cops mentioned a bank job I knew you'd done it.'

'It wasn't planned. We were in the disused toilets where they found your old man, digging a tunnel and there was a cave-in. The roof collapsed and he was still inside. There was nothing I could do. By the time I managed to get to him it was too late he was already dead.' Murphy lied like the professional he was.

'So you just went home and left him under a ton of bricks and forgot to tell Ma.' The younger man was getting angrier by the second.

Murphy drank deeply from the glass, inhibitions lowered. 'I panicked. There was feck all I could do, his head was bashed in. The shit was dead. I didn't know what to do, then I got to thinking, I couldn't tell anyone without dropping myself in the shit...so I left him.' The old man was thinking on his feet.

'Bastard,' was all Keane said.

'Your Ma was better off without him, and so were you.'

'I don't believe a word of it. If there had been an accident you'd have let on, not let Ma believe he'd done a runner.' Keane was steadily approaching his Uncle.

Murphy stepped back. He could smell Keane's stale breath. He was seeing a completely different side of his nephew. 'It's water under the bridge, lad. It was a long time ago, what happened, happened. I've always looked out for you haven't I? Forget it and move on,' he stepped back unsteadily.

'Just brush it under the carpet, carry on as if nothing's happened? Well I tell you what I think, Uncle Pat, I think you were jealous that Ma had a life. You couldn't bear the fact that someone else was looking out for her, she wouldn't need you anymore, so you topped him.'

Keane took a further step forward and Murphy edged backwards. He felt the edge of the large glass topped occasional table dig into the back of his legs. He lost balance staggering backwards. Instinctively he reached behind him with outstretched arms to try and save himself as the fragile surface gave way beneath him. His right arm encased in the fibre glass-cast was unable to support the weight of his body and the glass top shattered. Murphy lay twisted amongst the broken glass unable to move, His right arm lay at an odd angle, a sharp jagged shard dug deep, length ways, into the fleshy part of his left wrist, severing the veins completely.

'Can't move, lad, think something is stuck in my back. Christ, I'm bleeding like a stuffed pig. Give us a hand.' The deep pile carpet was quickly turning into a blood soaked sponge. Murphy began to lose consciousness.

Keane dropped to his knees, the blood continued to flow slowly from Murphy's wounds, soaking the already sodden carpet further. The old man was becoming paler, his breath rasped low, as life leached from his broken body. With his mobile in hand Keane fingered the keys, hesitated, fingers not moving as thoughts rushed through his head. The man groaning on the floor may be his Uncle, but he was also the same man who had murdered his father. He had deprived Keane of a father, a proper childhood, and his mother of a life with her husband. What if Murphy bled to death here on the floor in his own home, it was what he deserved, after all it had been an accident and no one could say otherwise. Keane shut down the mobile. He didn't make the call. He did hear his Uncle try to call his name as he left the room.

It wasn't an easy decision, but once made Keane didn't take a second glance at the old man lying on the sitting room floor. In the kitchen a strong fix of caffeine assisted Keane to gather his thoughts. Before he could call the emergency services there was one thing he had to bring to a conclusion.

***

'Excuse me, sir, you got a minute?' A young PC asked, popping his head around Marlowe's office door.

'A minute, that's all I've got.'

'It's Conway, I was taking him back to his cell and he said he wanted to speak to someone in charge and I can't get a hold of DI Gowan, sir.'

'What's he want?'

'Just said it was important, sir.'

In resignation, Marlowe eased back in his chair. 'Ok, get him back in an interview room, I'll be there shortly.' Wondering what it was all about, the DCI stood up from his desk, rubbed the twinge in his back and peered through the window into the squad room. The only person sat behind her desk was DC Etherington. He could just see the top of her head over the computer monitor. Marlowe wrapped his knuckles on the glass.

Tanya looked up, stopped what she was doing and walked across to the office. She knocked on the goldfish bowl door and opened it. 'Boss?' she said as she stuck her head around the door frame.

'Conway, he wants a word, grab us both a coffee and we'll go and see what he wants. And not from the vending machine,' he added as she disappeared, returning a few minutes later with two mugs of freshly brewed coffee.

Conway had been put back into the same room where his previous interview had taken place. The supervising officer stood by the door, while Conway occupied the same chair as previous. The DCI and Tanya entered the room, Tanya nodded, the officer acknowledged and left. This time there was no eagle eyed, plastic faced lawyer in sight.

'Gary, you wanted a word?' Marlowe said as he and Tanya sat down at the opposite side of the table.

'Yeah, well, I reckon I might have something that could help you.'

'What about your lawyer, don't you think he should be present to hear what you've got to say?' asked Tanya.

'Fuck him, tight faced twat.' This made Marlowe openly grin.

'Ok then, what have you got for us?'

'Oh no, not that easy. I want a deal.' Conway sat back in his chair, straight backed with his arms crossed.

'It doesn't work like that, Gary. We don't make deals, you've been watching too much television.' Marlowe was watching closely for any reaction. 'But what we can do is this, we can tell the Criminal Prosecution Service that you've been helpful and that you aided our case to bring about a favourable outcome. When you get to court, all the information you'll have given us can only stand you in good stead when it comes to sentencing. How does that sound?'

'Like a load of bollocks, but I don't have much choice do I?'

'It's entirely up to you, but I think it's as good as you're going to get.' It was Marlowe's turn to sit back...and wait for the response.

'Any chance of a cup of tea and a smoke?' asked Conway.

'The tea we can do,' Tanya replied looking towards the DCI, who nodded his head, 'the smoke maybe later.'

'Fair enough. Two sugars and plenty of milk.'

Tanya stood up, went to the door and called to the uniformed officer, who promptly returned a few minutes later with a full mug for Conway.

'Are you sure you don't want your lawyer present?' Marlowe asked the tea sipping bouncer.

'Don't think he'd like to hear what I'm going to say.'

'Ok,' Tanya switched on the tape recorder, stated the date, time, who was present in the interview room and more importantly that Gary Conway was still under caution and had refused further legal representation.

Marlowe opened the case file. 'Mr Conway, can you confirm where you work.'

'*The Snake Pit*, nightclub.'

'The same club owned by Mr Patrick Murphy and his nephew, Sean Keane.'

'That's the one,' confirmed Conway.

'Do you know Chas Logan, Ian Anderson and John Finch?' asked the DCI.

'Yeah, I know them, but I want it on record it wasn't me who topped Anderson, it was Murphy,' he stressed.

'But you did help dispose of the body?' Tanya asked.

'Well I had to didn't I?'

The fat bouncer went on to give chapter and verse, how Murphy came to recognise one of his attackers, Finch, and how finding his accomplices didn't give them any problems. He further described how he assisted Keane in the mutilations of Logan and Finch. Conway constantly stressed that he played no direct part in the murder of Anderson, but was responsible along with Keane for the dismemberment of Anderson's body.

'Now let's move on a little shall we?' Marlowe took a photograph of DC Kristianson from the folder and held it directly in front of the fat bouncers face. 'This man, have you seen him before?'

'Yep.' Conway sat back in his chair, he didn't need a second look.

174

'Yep... is that it?' Tanya blurted out.

'He was at the club wasn't he?' Fatty looked directly into Tanya's face. 'You should know, they tell me you were there as well.'

Marlowe looked at the clock, high on the wall. 'He's been missing for forty eight hours; can you throw any light as to his whereabouts?'

'Well if I was to give a well educated guess, I reckon he's where we dropped him off. In Mr Murphy's stable.'

Marlowe glanced at Tanya, then at the wall clock. 'Interview suspended at 2.48pm. He stood, gathered up his papers and was half-way out of the door before he'd finished speaking. Tanya escorted the fat bouncer to the custody area and followed Marlowe's booming voice to the squad room. 'Jonno, find the DI, we think we know where Lee is. Jenny I want an armed response team on stand-by.' Marlowe took out his cigarettes, brought the cigarette to his lips, changed his mind and stuffed it back in the packet. 'Tanya get all the available uniforms you can get hold of. Outside in five minutes.'

The DCI grabbed his jacket from the office and went out into the rear car park, now he could have that smoke. He paced the car park impatiently as he waited for the teams to gather. Marlowe knew it was against his better judgement going off half-cocked, no team briefing, no risk assessment, if he ended up getting his bollocks chewed off by the Super, so be it. His priority now was DC Lee Kristianson.

Chapter 31

No sound came from the study. Even so he closed the door quietly, as if not wanting to wake his Uncle. Using Murphy's keys he unlocked the steel gun cabinet, hidden away in the cupboard beneath the stairs. Keane selected a twelve gauge double barrelled shot gun and filled his pockets with cartridges, he didn't re-lock the cabinet. Back in the kitchen Keane took a bottle of cheap cooking brandy from the cupboard, unscrewed the cap and took a deep swallow from the bottle neck. With the bottle in one hand and the shotgun in the other, he opened the door leading to the back of the property and walked out.

Lee lay on his bed of straw, eyes closed, waiting for the next visit from Murphy, and wondering if it would be his last. The crunching of feet on gravel brought him back to reality. The young detective opened his eyes as Keane entered the stable. He hoped Murphy had the water bottle with him. It wasn't Murphy.

'You still with us then? I wasn't sure if Uncle Pat had dispatched you already. Want some?' Keane held up the bottle of brandy, moved across to where Lee was now in a kneeling position. 'You're going to need it.' Keane pushed the bottle neck into Lee's mouth and poured it down his throat, only stopping when Lee began to cough and splutter. 'That'll put hairs on your chest.' Lee shook his head as the fiery cheap booze burnt a trail down his throat to his stomach. The overspill ran down his chin and neck.

Keane stood the bottle down on the floor and walked to where the tack was kept. He took down a coil of rope they used for making temporary pens for the ponies. He dropped the rope to the floor, released the chain from around the cleat holding the overhead hoist in place. Hand over hand the chain was fed through the block and tackle, bringing the hook of the hoist that had held Anderson, down to shoulder height. 'Don't look so worried,' he chided Lee. Before Lee could respond a dirty rag was stuffed in his mouth, making him gag. Keane once again picked up the rope and fashioned an effective looking slip knot. A noose.

He retrieved the bottle and brought it to his mouth and drank deep. 'Come on, on your feet.' Lee remained kneeling. 'Don't fuck me about,' he took a handful of Lee's hair and dragged him upwards, 'ups-a-daisy.' Lee didn't realise how weak he was. The pain in his legs was excruciating as he felt the blood rush down his legs to his feet, causing him to stumble against Keane. 'You've picked a right fucking time to get amorous.' Keane laughed out loud at his own joke. 'Come on let me help you,' he slipped the noose around Lee's neck and made it fast around the hoist hook, grabbed the chain and began to pull hand over hand, raising the young DC into the standing position.

Lee struggled. The attempt was futile, legs taped together at the ankles and his hands fixed behind his back. Keane retrieved his bottle and held it high. 'To you and Uncle fucking Pat, cheers,' he toasted and drank from the bottle. 'Right, I'm going to cut the tape round your ankles, and believe me if you try anything you'll wish you fucking hadn't.' Keane took the well used trimming knife from his pocket and eased out the retractable blade, holding the knife where Lee could see it. 'Good knife this, you ask Finchy or Logan, they'll tell you it's fucking lethal. Now keep still.' With one swift movement the knife flashed downwards. 'Whoops,' the knife sliced the tape, along with Lee's sock. Lee groaned loudly through his rag filled mouth, as the blood from his ankle flowed into his shoe. 'Right up you go,' Keane kicked Lee in the injured ankle. 'Stand on that bale.' Good leg first he wobbled as he tried to support his weight and drag the other bloody foot up onto the bale of straw. Keane again pulled on the chain, the noose tightened around Lee's neck as the rope became taut. Keane dropped the chains, picked up the bottle and downed what was remaining. That's when he heard movement outside the stable. 'Don't go anywhere.' The bottle was replaced with the shotgun. He broke the breach and slipped in two cartridges. Click, the gun was closed and the safety catch released.

The atmosphere was tense. Officers stood in small groups, waiting for instructions. 'Are we ready?' Marlowe asked Dave Gowan, as he took a last drag of the cigarette and dropped the butt to the floor, grinding it out with his foot.

Gowan walked over, plastic cup of coffee in his hand. 'All set, boss.'

'What about the armed response?'

'Already dispatched.' He binned the coffee cup.

'You tell them to keep well back 'til we get there?'

'Told them to wait at the edge of the village.'

'That's it then, we're off.'

With blues and two's blaring, the small convoy headed out of the car park towards the village of Ellerton along the A63, Clive Sullivan Way. Traffic was relatively light, not that it would have mattered with the convoy blaring a path through the vehicles. Ten minutes later they approached Ellerton. As instructed, the armed response team in an un-marked white van was parked up in a lay-by on the edge of the village.

The vehicles became soundless as they passed the armed response van. The white van joined on the tail of the convoy. Dave Gowan took his AirWaves radio from his jacket, and pressed the talk button. 'Silent approach, get that? Silent approach.'

Some two hundred metres from Murphy's detached home, the vehicles came to a stop. Marlowe gathered the team leaders and confirmed their instructions and made doubly sure that the plain clothes officers were wearing their protective-vests. He didn't want any accidents from stray bullets. The teams scattered around the near-by properties making their approaches. The armed response team positioned themselves strategically around the house and the stable block, every angle was covered.

Marlowe was torn, should he just have the front door battered down with steel enforcer or take a stealthier approach. He went for the former. A burly uniformed officer stood facing the front door. The door was well constructed from hard-wood. The officer looked towards Marlowe who nodded his head. The metal enforcer was swung back in an arc, smash, it hit the lock…back again, crash, the timber around the lock gave way and the door swung inwards.

'Police,' Dave Gowan screamed out as the team entered the hall way. No response, again he yelled out 'Police,' again silence.

Marlowe couldn't believe they hadn't met any resistance. 'Ok, you two, to the nearest uniforms, 'upstairs, Jonno, go with them.' Feet thumped their way up the stairs, two at a time.

'This is too good to be bloody true,' Marlowe said to Dave Gowan as the teams spread through the house. Boots pounded through every room in the house.

'Sir, in here,' Tanya shouted with urgency. Marlowe and Gowan found her in the conservatory, kneeling on the floor next to the contorted bloody body of Patrick Murphy, who lay in an expanding crimson pool.

'Bloody hell. Is he still alive?' asked the DCI.

'Looks past his sell by-date, if you ask me,' Gowan said as flippant as ever.

'No pulse.' Tanya replied as she held a latex covered hand to Murphy's neck.

'Get the FME down here, and the CSEs.' Marlowe said over his shoulder to whoever was listening in.

'Accident?' asked Gowan.

'From the look of it yes, but best wait for the Doc before we jump to conclusions.' Marlowe walked across the room and looked out of the picture-window facing the rear of the property. He took the AirWaves from his pocket. 'What's happening?' he said into the handset requesting an update from the firearms team.

'All quiet, sir. The perimeter of the stable's secure. No sign of movement,' replied the armed response team leader. 'Scrap that, just heard movement inside.'

'Ok, on my way, stand-by 'till I get there.'

Keane swayed. The cheap brandy had achieved the desired effect, with alcohol induced heightened senses he was still in control and aware of activity in the paddock. 'You just hang around a mo,' he said to Lee as he chanced a look through the side door. 'Shit!' The armed officer raised his weapon and Keane slammed the door shut. 'Now what are we going to do, not that you're going to do anything.' Lee wasn't in any position to try and talk him down, Keane began to get hyper. 'It's all your own fault.' Lee cringed as Keane poked and prodded with the barrel of shotgun. The safety catch was still in the off position, the young detective shuddered. 'If you'd kept that bleedin' nose of yours out of what doesn't concern you, we wouldn't be in this situation.' Keane kicked out at the bale of straw Lee stood on. He froze expecting the worse and waited for the noose to tighten. It didn't happen. 'Bastards, bastards,' Keane picked up the brandy bottle and swallowed down the last of the cheap alcohol.

***

Outside, they could hear the smash of the glass as Keane hurled the bottle against the wall.

'How many men have you got in position?' Marlowe asked the Armed Response Commander.

'Six. All windows and exits covered. The double doors are locked with a padlock on the outside, so I reckon the side door is favourite if he tries to make a break for it. I have officers in position, ready to take him out should it come to it,' he inclined his head towards the single timber door.

'What do you think our chances would be if we rushed the place?'

'Not an option. We know it's more than probable he's armed, but the question is what state of mind is he in? Would he use the firearm?'

'Oh yes, I think he'd use it, the question is would he use it on Lee?'

'I suggest we sit tight and get a negotiator down here,' the commander suggested.

'I agree. Dave, get it sorted ASAP.'

Dave Gowan, clicked his AirWaves and made the request. He walked away towards the side of the house where the rest of the plain clothes officers were waiting for instructions. 'What's happening?' Tanya asked as soon as he turned the corner of the building.

'There's not a lot to tell. There's some noise from inside but...' he shrugged his shoulders.

'Do we know if Lee's alright?'

'Again, I don't know.' Gowan glanced over his shoulder towards the paddock.

'Can't the armed response rush the place?'

He shook his head. 'Just got to play the waiting game.'

'Yeah I know, sorry.' Tanya felt foolish for asking.

'We're waiting for Central to send a negotiator, hope he doesn't take all bloody day to get here.'

Gowan's handset "blipped" an incoming call. 'Dave, we've got movement in the stables,' Marlowe told him in a whispered voice. The stable door was ajar when Gowan reached the controlled area. He was just in time to see the barrel of a shotgun pushed through the gap between the door and frame. A moment later it was withdrawn back through the space.

Keane once again began the pacing. 'Shit.' He kicked out at the pieces of broken glass. 'Suppose it's time to get on with it, what do you reckon?' Keane said waving the shotgun around like a toy. 'Too much water under the bridge - can't get back from this one and I'm not spending the next fifteen years in the lock-up.' Keane levelled the shotgun at Lee's chest.

Lee's chest heaved in and out as if he'd ran a marathon race, any second he was expecting to be flung off the straw bale by a hail of shotgun pellets. 'Too easy,' said Keane. Lee's breathing eased slightly at the reprieve.

Unexpectedly, Keane swung out with the barrel of the gun and caught the back of Lee's legs making them buckle. The young DC swung like a marionette on the end of the rope, his legs kicking frantically trying to find purchase on the bale. Keane ran towards the door, with the shotgun held at waist height pointing forward, he swung open the door and stopped dead in his tracks as three red laser beam point found their target. He looked down at the circle of lights on his chest, laughed and ran out, letting go with both barrels as he did. Knocked six feet backwards by three shells from Heckler & Koch G3 Sniper Rifles, Keane was already dead by the time he fell to the floor.

After the gun shots there was silence. No one moved until a lone, armed officer stepped cautiously forward. It was obvious Keane was dead, but this was when the training kicked in. 'Area secure,' he yelled as he picked up the discharged weapon from the floor.

Lee struggled desperately and managed to place the toes of his good foot on the edge of the bale. He balanced precariously. His leg muscles tightened, he didn't know how long he would be able to keep the position.

Marlowe didn't waste time, he was through the stable door within seconds, right on his heels were Gowan, Tanya and Jonno. Instinctively he grabbed the young detective around the legs, holding and lifting at the same time, trying to create some slackness in the rope. Jonno helped the DCI take the weight, grabbing Lee around his waist. Gowan grabbed the chain and pulled arm over arm as fast as he could. It seemed to take forever before Lee was gradually lowered to the floor.

'Medics, we need the paramedics in here now,' Tanya yelled over her shoulder.

There was no need. The paramedics were right behind her. The first team stepped over the bloodied body of Sean Keane and went to the aid of the young detective, the latter dropped to their knees by the dead body in their path. Not that there was anything they could do. Marlowe took a step back, watching as the paramedics fixed an oxygen mask to Lee and set about their examination. Leaving Tanya kneeling by Lee's side and knowing the young detective was now in the safe hands of the professionals, Marlowe walked away from the organised chaos of the stables.

He needed some quiet time. Standing at the edge of the paddock, with a cigarette between his lips he wondered if things could have been done differently, he guessed not. Watching people die a violent death was not a thing Marlowe would ever get used to. Not even Sean Keane getting his deserved reward would change that. There were no two ways about it, the DCI was pleased that DC Kristianson had been found alive, injured but still there to tell the tale. But the young detective was in for the rollicking of a lifetime after he'd been checked out. He stubbed his cigarette out in the mud and made his way back to the activity within the house.

'How's it going in here,' he shouted as he placed a foot in the kitchen.

'Getting there,' Jonno answered. The bagged up body of Murphy was being wheeled away on trolley.

'This might cheer you up, boss,' Jenny held up a parcel in her hand, it was the package of Heroin that had gone missing.

'Nice one. Now all we've got to do is find out who nicked it in the first place, and woe-betide whoever it was when I get hold of them.' Marlowe stood looking around. A job well done, but he was far from happy. He stood savouring the moment.

'The negotiator is here,' a voice called out.

'Well tell him to sod off again.'

END

About the Author

Alfie Robins was born and raised in the English east coast city of Kingston Upon Hull, known locally as, 'Ull. Alfie left school at 15 and started work as a ships carpenter working on the trawlers on Hull fish dock. Over the years he has had a varied career, carpenter, production manager in the caravan industry and sales manager with a radio communications company, to name but a few. He is now retired and concentrates on his writing.

Alfie has three grown up children and lives with his wife, son and two rabbits in East Yorkshire, England.

If you enjoyed this book

you may like the following titles by Alfie Robins

Reprisal

Some of the most vibrant and varied crime writing around anywhere is centered on the evocative industrial fishing port of Hull, with its shadowy wind-swept streets, its hard-bitten attitudes, its drugs, its gangsters and yet its underlying humanity that clings like untended weeds amid the cracks of the endemic poverty and the violence.

And Alfie Robins' 'Reprisal' is an outstanding example of the genre, a classic police procedural where you can hear the streets, smell the weather, savour the taciturn banter, and feel the four inch nail being driven into the heads of victims by a vengeful, meticulous and psychotic serial killer.

This is a criminal environment as real as it gets, and this is how people die if DCI Philip Marlowe and his over-stretched, tight-knit team don't get there first.

Just Whistle

My name is John Osbourne; well it was before I started writing this bloody book, now I'm not sure who the hell I am. If you think you know me, please telephone 01482 21...

Unemployed and recently divorced, John Osbourne's life was slowly falling apart, then, encouraged to get a hobby by his daughter things took a different turn, a turn that he did not realise would change his life. As he starts writing his first novel, the characters seem to come alive before his very eyes.

Osbourne's creation, Detective Sergeant Harry "H" Blackburn and his team find themselves involved in the investigation of the murder of a young female student which leads them to the dangerous world of drug trafficking. When their only witness is murdered it becomes even more difficult for the team to get justice.

As the lines between reality and fiction blur, Osbourne struggles to maintain his grip on reality as he enters the realm of fiction
Will Harry and the team get their man, but if they do, will John Osbourne be lost in the world of fiction forever?

Lightning Source UK Ltd.
Milton Keynes UK
UKOW04f2039290714

235959UK00001B/57/P